adp

THE DISTINCTION OF THE MATURE AND THE HORROR OF THE NAIVE

AND OTHER STORIES OF YOUTH IN LIMBO

THE DISTINCTION OF THE MATURE AND THE HORROR OF THE NAIVE

AND OTHER STORIES OF YOUTH IN LIMBO

ELLISON FOWLER

The Artless Dodges Press
www.TheArtlessDodgesPress.com
Cleveland, Ohio

The Distinction of the Mature and the Horror of the Naive
and Other Stories of Youth in Limbo
collected short stories by Ellison Fowler
ISBN 0981993966
EAN-13 9780981993966
copyright © 2011 Artless Dodges, Inc.
Published by The Artless Dodges Press
Cleveland, Ohio
www.TheArtlessDodgesPress.com

Cover design by T. Maven
www.TrashMaven.WordPress.com

Contents

Papa

Pretty much the whole time I've known George, he's been talking me into things.

I've known George since I was five, since his family moved in down the street from us. That means I've known him for more than two-thirds of my life. My little sister was born when I was six, so I've known George longer than I've known her. The whole time, he's been getting me to do things I wouldn't ordinarily do.

The thing about George is, he's a little bit crazy. The reason George's family moved in down the street from me is, George's dad got transferred at work. But then, six months later, George's dad got transferred again. George's mom refused to move, though, because they'd just moved, so George's dad got an apartment near the other office, in another city. He lived there all week and then came home on weekends. We were just kids, then, so we didn't know all of what was going on.

After his dad moved to be near the other office, George went a little bit crazy. What I mean is, he started doing things that were a little bit nuts. He started stealing things, but he always stole things that didn't make any sense. He would sneak up to houses and steal bird feeders and garden hoses. One time I asked him what he did with everything, and because I was his best friend he took me way out into the woods behind his house and showed me a place that nobody else knew about, a place that had been quarried out and then got filled up with rainwater. It made a kind of pond back there, and George threw everything he stole into it. I asked him why he would go through so much trouble to steal things and then just throw them into the quarry, and he just shrugged and looked annoyed that I didn't understand, like it was my fault. After that I didn't ask anymore, and whenever anyone talked about George when he wasn't around I would act annoyed that they didn't understand, like it was their fault. But I didn't understand either, and I still don't.

Everybody knew this about George. Not where he put the things, I mean, but that he stole things and did things that didn't make any sense to anyone else. It's the kind of thing that can make living in a town the size of ours absolutely impossible, and it probably would have been worse for him except that all of a sudden, in eighth grade, he became fantastically good at sports. It was like one day it just clicked for him, what everyone had been doing in the gym and out in the fields behind the school. He walked into the wrestling room and started dumping guys on their heads, guys who had been wrestling for years. All of a sudden he became one of those guys who plays a sport every season. I guess his parents had been on him to get involved with sports. They figured it would keep him from getting any worse, from doing anything any crazier. At this point in the history of parenting, it seems like a pretty standard move. His way of getting back at them was to do every single sport he could. I think it was his way of showing them how stupid and cliched it was for them to want him to get involved in sports, like it was 1950 and all he needed was some school spirit and and some exercise. Like I said, George is a little bit crazy.

He says, "When we're having a pep rally, all I can think about is running down on the field and fucking all the cheerleaders, all at once. That's how much pep I've got."

"Jesus Christ," I say, and I laugh and I shake my head, and I sort of watch him because even though I know he won't do it, with George you never really know that he won't do it.

George is my best friend. I've known him longer than I've known anybody else, except my parents. My parents don't think George is crazy, but they've known George for as long as I have. Whenever I say that he's crazy and I tell them something he said or did they just sort of shrug and look at me like I don't understand something that I will when I'm older, something that they can't make me understand because it takes experience or age or something. I don't tell them any of the really crazy stuff he says or does, though, so I always figure that if they heard what he really did they would agree with me. But it's probably good that they don't know how crazy George is, because if they did then they never would have let me go on this trip.

George says, "Tell them it's a cultural exchange. Tell them we're going to go to a bunch of museums. Tell them I'm thinking of majoring in art history. People our parents' age can't resist culture."

I say, "Shut up, George," because my parents are coming to talk to us in a minute and I don't want him to screw it up.

When I explain the trip my father says, "How are you going to pay for everything?"

George says, "I'm going to pay for it. I've been saving up. At the end we're going to figure out how much everything cost and he's going to pay me back half."

My father says, "You've been saving up," and it isn't a question. He repeats things back to you when he wants you to know how unlikely they sound.

But George says, "Yeah. My grandparents give me money for my birthday and for Christmas every year. They've got lots of money and they're totally senile. Plus, sometimes I do these landscaping jobs in the summer, between baseball and football season. You can make a lot of money landscaping."

"Uh huh," says my father. Then he turns to me and says, "And how are you going to pay him back? You're going to be in school in the fall. Do you think you'll have time for a job, too?"

"Sure," I say. "I think so," even though I have absolutely no idea.

"It's ok, anyway," says George. "He can pay me back whenever. It's totally fine."

My father looks at my mother and says, "We have to talk about this," and it's like somebody putting forty pounds of sand on my shoulders. George doesn't even miss a beat, though. He smiles and gets up, like he's made his offer and like he thinks the meeting went really well, and now he's going to go back to the office and wait for the go-ahead.

I say, "It's only a couple of weeks. And there are lots of hostels. It's totally safe. Over there people do it all the time. You can even pick up hitchhikers."

My mother says, "Good God, don't even think about hitchhiking."

And my father holds up a hand and says, "Beth, we will talk about it," speaking very slowly and softly, in his conflict-avoidance voice.

I'm going to say something else but George takes hold of my arm and when I look at him he just nods like he knows what he's doing and we go outside. Once we're outside he tells me to cool it, because he can see that I'm really upset. He tells me that we just have to show them that we're adults just like them, and that we can handle this. We have to let them know that this is something that people do. He tells me just to calm down and to trust him. I tell him that I do trust him, and I really do, because even though he's a little bit crazy he always seems to know exactly what he's doing.

A week later I'm in the kitchen with George and my parents come in together and my dad says your mother and I have been talking and we've decided that you're an adult now and our conditions are and blah blah blah and I agree to everything they say because they've said yes and nothing else matters, and because I want this more than I've ever wanted anything else in my entire life.

It's not until we're on the plane that George tells me we're not doing all of the stuff we've been talking about doing, all of the stuff we've been telling my parents we're doing, because we're going to Pamplona for the Festival de San Fermin, that we're going to run with the bulls, and he's already booked our train tickets.

"Well you can unbook them," I say. "You can cancel them. You can get your money back. I'm serious, George. I'm completely dead serious. My parents barely let me go on this trip. I don't even want to think about what they'd do if they found out we did this."

"I can't," says George. "I can't unbook them." And then he doesn't say anything else, like that's the final word, like there's nothing else to say about it.

"Jesus, George," I say. "Seriously. What the hell?" And I turn and face the window to show him how pissed I am.

"Come on," George says. "Come on, don't be pissed. You know you're not really pissed at me. You know you didn't want to go look at museums and old buildings. Did you really care about waiting in line for two hours to go up the Eiffel Tower?"

And I say, "Just shut up for a second. Stop talking for a second." But I'm not even surprised, because I've known George long enough that I should have guessed that he was planning something like this. I've known George long enough to know that this was coming. For a minute I'm not even pissed that he didn't tell me, not even pissed that he changed our plans without even bothering to ask me. For a minute I'm just pissed at him for being so goddamned sure of himself, so sure that he can talk me into it. And I'm pissed that he's right to be confident about it, because even before I start to argue with him I know I'm going to go along with it.

"Look," he says, "my parents would be just as pissed as yours if they found out. They'd probably be more pissed. They're not going to find out, OK? We'll figure it out. They're not going to find out." Then he says, "I really can't cancel the tickets. I asked the lady when I bought them. I guess we could just waste them, but they were really expensive."

I say, "How expensive?" and he tells me. "Jesus, George," I say again, still looking out the window. The ocean is way down below us, and I start thinking about how much there is to the ocean, and how there are still parts of it we haven't explored, and fish we haven't discovered. But I only think this because I'm looking at the water, and I'm only looking at the water because I know that when I turn back George will start talking, and he won't stop until I've agreed. I don't want to argue with him and I don't want to agree with him and all of a sudden I'm exhausted and annoyed with him for putting me in this position, for putting me in this position over and over again for the entire time I've known him. So I say, without looking at him, "Just leave me alone, OK? Don't talk to me for like, an hour. Just let me think about it."

"All right," says George. "That's fine. OK," and that's the last thing he says to me for a solid hour. Like it's a deal we just made. Like if he doesn't say anything for an hour then I'll agree to go along with whatever he's planning. Like I'm going to be just that easy to win over.

So after an hour I say, "Are they serving a meal on this flight?" because I know it's killing George to wait for me to come back with an answer.

"I don't know," he says. "Do you want me to ask?"

And I look around for a long minute before I say, without looking at him, like I'm doing him a favor just talking to him, "No, it's cool. It doesn't matter." But after I say this I can't think of anything else to say to keep him from asking me, because after all we had a deal and it's been an hour. So just so I don't have to give him the satisfaction I say, before he can ask me, "All right. But I want to know what we're doing. I want to be part of the plan, from now on. Don't sneak around changing things on me all the time. It's not cool."

"Totally," says George. "Absolutely. Absolutely."

We take a train from Heathrow to Paddington Station, then another train from Paddington Station to Paris. Then we take an overnight train from Paris to Barcelona, and then another train from Barcelona to Pamplona. I barely sleep at all on the train. We take a cab from the station into town and the driver speaks English and tells us that we should be going to the campground, not into town, and that there isn't going to be anywhere to stay. This makes sense to me and I tell George that I think so, but George looks at me like my agreeing is just as bad as not wanting to come here in the first place. I figure that George has the money and so he can do what he wants, and if I can't convince him of anything then it's not worth the effort. I'm tired from not sleeping and anxious that we're here and anxious because I have to call my parents to let them know that I'm OK, because I forgot to call them in London. I'm going to have to tell them that's where I am, and it makes me nervous because I never got very good at lying to them.

The driver lets us off in front of a white brick building. There are tables set up outside and people sitting around drinking and through the windows I see more people inside. I say that it looks like a bar and the driver tells us that there are rooms upstairs, and that since it's not a hotel, more like a bar that's sort of a hotel, a lot of the tourists coming in don't know about it, and we have a better chance of finding a room. George pays the driver and we go inside, and George tells me to hang back while he goes and talks to the bartender. I do. It's hot and I'm wearing my backpack, and I can feel sweat running down the small of my back. I'm too nervous about getting a room and about calling my parents to even be excited. But then, after about ten minutes, George comes back over and he's smiling and carrying a bottle of wine and he says it's all straightened out, no problem, and he's got a room for us.

"How?" I say as we're going up the stairs.

George says, "Don't worry about it."

"No, really," I say, "how?"

George says, "I charmed him. I'm a charming guy."

"You probably payed double," I say. "Shit, you probably payed triple."

George says, "It's bad juju to talk about money at a time like this."

We get up to the room. The room is really small - there's just enough room to walk between the bed and the walls and the dresser - but it has it's own bathroom, with a shower stall and everything. I wonder what George payed for it and then I decide not to worry about it. I think the bartender probably was holding it for someone else, but gave it to George when he saw that he could get more for it. I think about how pissed whoever was supposed to get the room is going to be, when they get here and the bartender tells them that their room is gone. I wonder if we're going to come back and find all of our stuff in the hall and somebody else in the room, and then I decide again that I'm not going to worry about it. George opens the window and a breeze comes in and I hear the people in the street below yelling to each other and singing in Spanish and it's like something out of a novel or a movie and for a second I can only feel how much better this is than anything else I've ever experienced.

"We should call home," I say. "I forgot to call in London."

"Sure," says George. "I should, too. We'll go find a phone."

We take one of the bottles with us and go looking for a phone. The streets are crowded and everyone is talking loud and singing and calling to one another. We find a pay phone down one of the streets and I call with a calling card my parents gave me before I left. They're not home, though, so I leave a message and I say I'm in London and that we're at the hostel and everything is fine and I'll try them again later. While I'm talking I cup my hand around the mouthpiece because I'm worried that they'll hear everyone yelling in Spanish, but I tell myself that probably it'll just sound like noise. Then George calls his parents, and they're not home either, and he leaves them a message saying pretty much the same thing.

Walking away from the phone booth I feel a lot better. We start drinking from the bottle and pretty soon we've finished it, and so we stop in at a bar and buy another. George pays. He's got a huge wad of bills he changed at Heathrow. I ask him how much he has and he says not to worry about it. I tell him it's stupid to carry around all of our money in cash and that, since I'm sure that he knows how stupid that would be, I'm sure that he isn't carrying all of our money around in cash, on him, all the time. He laughs and tells me to lighten up and not worry so much, which is something he has been telling for years.

I say, "Every time you tell me to lighten up it means you're planning on us doing something you know I think we shouldn't do."

George says, "Life is going to happen to you whether you worry about it or not. There's nothing you can do about anything that's coming your way. You're just wasting your own time and energy, wondering what it's going to be."

And because I'm young, and I still think in a way I won't later that the things people say where they're drunk can be profound and insightful, and because I'm drunk too and in a new place and I feel like I'm seeing life for the first time, I say, "You're right. You're absolutely right," and I'm so glad that I'm here with George and so glad that he's my best friend.

It's dark by the time we get down to the ring. We're standing in front of the bust of Hemingway that they've got mounted on pedestal in a little grotto outside, and George is peeing on the base of the pedestal. He's laughing about it and I'm laughing too, and some people walk by and yell at us in Spanish. But they don't stop, and so neither do we. We just keep laughing.

George says, "I really hated *Old Man and the Sea*," and I don't say anything because now I'm laughing too hard to talk. George says, "The whole time I was supposed to be reading it, my dad kept telling me about how Hemingway had changed his life. He said Hemingway changed his view of what it meant to be a man."

I say, "No offense, but I don't see your dad as the Hemingway type."

"I know," says George. "Neither do I. Neither does anybody. That's what made it such a stupid thing to say." He's finished and he zips up and comes back over and takes the bottle from me. He's not laughing anymore and I want to apologize for saying that his dad wasn't Hemingway, because it seems like it upset him even though he agreed.

I say, "I'm sorry."

George says, "For what?"

I say, "For saying that. About your dad."

George says, "You can be as sorry as you want, it doesn't change the fact that my dad is no Hemingway." And he laughs again, but it's kind of forced. But I'm drunk and I want it to be OK, so I laugh too. Then George says, "Let's go back to the bar and see if we can find any girls who speak English."

The bar at the place we're staying is crowded and loud. Someone hands George a bottle as we come through the door and George takes it and drinks from it and then hands it to me. I go to refuse but the woman who handed it to George makes a face like she'd be hurt if I did. So I drink and George says something that I can't hear over the noise.

I say, "What?"

George yells, "Nothing. Never mind. I'll tell you later. Remind me."

I'm wondering what he said, but I have the sense that sooner or later I'm going to wish he hadn't told me. It's just one of those things with George. Like coming here in the first place. Not that you hate his idea, just that things were going along and could have kept going along. But now they won't. So I say, "I think I'm going to go up. The noise is giving me a headache."

George nods and says, "I'll be up soon."

I go upstairs and go into our room. I leave George the bed and I lay down on the floor with one of the pillows. It's hot in the room and the breeze coming in through the window is hot, too, and from the street outside I can hear voices and laughter and yelling and music. I lay awake for a while and then when it doesn't look like George is coming I climb up onto the bed and lay facedown with a pillow over my head to block out the noise.

I guess I fall asleep, then, because I wake up when I hear George coming in. I hear him set three bottles down on the table next to the door and I say, "How was it down there?"

He says, "Good. I brought some more wine."

I say, "Good." George sits down on the foot of the bed and then he lays down across my legs and feet and I laugh and kick at him and say, "Get off me, man. It's hot enough in here already."

But he doesn't move. He stays laying across my legs and says, "You should have seen the girl I was dancing with."

"Yeah?" I say.

"Yeah," says George. "Beautiful."

I say, "Then why aren't you sleeping in her room, instead of across my legs?"

George says, "You'd miss me."

I say, "Not likely."

George says, "You would. Think about how much you would miss me, if I wasn't here to make you do all the things you wouldn't have the balls to do on your own. You wouldn't even know what you were missing."

"Oh yeah," I say. "I can think of a couple of things."

Then neither of us says anything for a while. We just lay there in the dark, me on the bed and George laying across my legs. Then George says, "Hey listen man, I'm really glad we did this. I'm really glad, you know, that we took this trip."

I say, "Me too."

And George says, "Because, you know, we've been best friends for a long time, and I think it would be really lame if we went off to school next year without a big tour of... I don't know. Mayhem and craziness."

"I totally agree," I say. "It wouldn't be right."

"Right," says George. Then I think he's going to say something, but he doesn't. Then he says, "All right man. I'll talk to you in the morning." But he doesn't move, he just sort of presses down harder on my legs. And so I start trying to get my legs out from underneath him, but the more I do the more he presses down on them. Then I start really kicking, really trying to shake him, and he turns so that he's holding my legs with his arms. We're both laughing and I'm kicking and I say, "Get off me, you asshole."

And he says, "Make me."

And I say, "Fine," and I sit up and I start pushing him. But he just hangs on tighter, and we start shaking the bed and it's banging against the wall and we start laughing because we're probably waking up the people in the next room. Then George moves a little bit and I manage to get both feet against his ribs and I push him with both legs, and he goes flying off the bed and in the wall, so hard that he leaves a big dented imprint in the plaster. I switch on the light and we both look at it, and then George starts laughing again and I start laughing, too and I say, "They're going to be so pissed at us," and then we laugh a lot harder.

George says, "You would miss me. You would totally miss me."

And I say, "Keep telling yourself that."

He says, "You know. You won't admit it, but you know you would."

I say, "Go to sleep."

George wakes me up early. He says, "We've got to hurry. We should have been there ten minutes ago." He says, "I already opened the wine. Better drink it before we go."

I say, "We can just take it with us."

George shakes his head and says, "We don't want to be carrying glass. Just see if you can finish off the bottle. We've got to get moving." He puts the half-emptied bottle in my hands and I tip it back. The wine tastes sour first thing in the morning and George says, "That's good. That's really good. You'll feel better once it's down." I stop drinking with a quarter of the bottle left and groan and George says, "It's the way God intended you to wake up."

I take a deep breath and then finish the bottle and I say, "I'm going to throw up."

George says, "You're fine." He says, "Let's move."

We leave the room and go downstairs. The bar is almost empty and I feel the wine start to work its way back up my insides as George pushes through the door and starts running. I follow him, but after a hundred feet

I give up and start walking. The sun is already hot and I can hear the crowd ahead of us. George yells for me to hurry and I start running again, and we come around the corner into the courtyard in front of the town hall just as the first rocket goes up, and I think how the men in their white shirts and pants and red sashes look just like the picture in the guidebook as they turn and start running toward us.

George grabs me by the shoulders and turns me, and we start running with the crowd as they reach us and the second rocket goes up. Then the other runners and the noise from the other runners are all around me and I can't tell if the pounding and breathing close behind me is the people or the bulls. I keep running and the wine is burning in my stomach, and I see George as he pulls ahead and then turns back to look at me, to make sure I'm all right. Then he starts to slow and I slow with him, and people start moving past us and bumping into us and I hear cursing in Spanish and then some in English and other languages and then George is beside me and I say, "What are you doing?"

He says, "I want to see the bulls."

We're almost running in place, with everyone moving around us. Then I see the first bull, and I start running hard again and I don't turn around anymore. All around me I can hear people yelling and I'm not sure what it means and I'm not sure if it's the people behind the barricades or the people in the street. Then the ring is up ahead and I feel a hand on my shoulder and it's George and he pulls himself past me and pushes off and

I stumble and almost fall. I watch him duck a shoulder and slide between two men and then I can't see him anymore and I yell after him. Then I start running hard again, because I can hear the hooves on the street behind me, and then I am inside and the corridor leading into the ring is close with the bodies. Then I am through and I move fast to one side and jump the barricade, and then climb the wall and lay where I fall beneath the seats. I lay with my eyes closed and listen to the bulls hit the walls and the men yelling. Then someone kicks me in the ribs and I look up and it's George.

He says, "How was it for you?"

I close my eyes and say, "Terrible. I thought you were going to leave me back there, you asshole. I thought you were going to let me get trampled to death."

George says, "I wouldn't do that. I'd have to tell your parents." He sits down and waits for me to catch my breath. After a while I sit up and George slaps me on the back.

Down in the ring, the bulls have calmed down. The runners are over the barricades, and the people in the stands have stopped cheering. George pulls me to my feet and we sidestep our way down the aisle to the stairs and then down the corridor with the crowd and out into the street.

We have breakfast at a café, but we have to eat it standing up near the back wall because the place is so crowded. George eats his breakfast and then what's left of mine because I can't get most of it down. He looks me over and then shakes his head and says, "You've got to pull it together."

I say, "I'm fine. I just need a minute to rest. I just need to get my bearings. Give me the keys. I'm going back to the room."

George hands me the key. He says, "That's a good idea. Get some sleep. I'll come get you in a few hours. I'll see if I can find out what's else is going on."

I leave the café and go back to the room, but I can't sleep. I lay awake for a while. My heart is still pounding. The room is hot and I sweat into the sheets and I can smell the alcohol leeching out of me. Finally I get up and open one of the two bottles we have left and take a few big drinks. Then I lay down, and wait for it to hit me. After it does I feel better, and the heat doesn't bother me as much, and I fall asleep.

George comes in a few hours later. He's got a girl with him, and I think that she's probably Spanish. Her hair is black and her skin is dark. She looks drunk but she looks more tired than drunk. She leans on the open door and closes her eyes as George comes into the room and starts going through my backpack.

George says, "Time to get up." He throws something at me and says, "Put this on."

I sit up and pull the tee-shirt over my head and the girl says, "Can I have some of this wine?" and her voice is very American and not at all Spanish.

George says, "Sure." He says, "*Fiesta. Fee-YES-tah Feeeeee-YES-tah!*"

I say, "What time is it?"

The girl says, "Can I open this other bottle?"

George says, "There's a corkscrew on the table." He is sitting in a low squat on the floor, holding my backpack open, and I see the wad of cash he carries in his right front pocket peeking out. Then, as he moves, it falls out and I don't say anything because I want to see if he'll notice. The girl is working the cork out of the bottle and when it comes some of the wine splashes on her hand and she licks it off.

George says, "Where's the other shirt I brought?"

I say, "How should I know?" I have my legs over the side of the bed and my head hurts. The girl comes around behind George and squats down behind him, wrapping her arms around his neck. George takes the bottle from her and as he drinks she picks up the money and holds it behind his back.

George stops drinking and says, "Money?"

And I say, "She's got it."

And she laughs and says, "And I'm never giving it back." She rolls onto her back as George turns and George lunges for it and lands on top of her, between her legs. She crosses her ankles behind his back while she laughs and holds the money high out above her head. She says, "Sorry, it's mine now."

He says, "Give it back."

She laughs and says, "Mine now." She pushes him with her free hand and George flops to the side and they roll over, so that she ends up on top of him, and they almost knock the bottle over.

I say, "Watch the wine, would you? For Christ's sake watch the wine." Then I get up and pick up the bottle and I take the money from the girl's hand. I say, "Mine now."

The girl says, "No fair."

George says, "Have another drink."

The girl pouts and rocks back onto George's hips. She is wearing a lavender-colored dress that drapes over George's chest. George lifts the front of it and looks underneath and the girl slaps his hand and says, "No peeking."

George says, "Just a little peek."

The girl closes her eyes and sways. She says, "What about your friend?"

I say, "Jesus Christ." I say, "I'll be down in the bar."

George says, "Thanks." He says, "I owe you one."

I stuff the money into my pocket and take the bottle I started and I close the door behind me. I stop on the landing and finish the bottle, and then I leave the bottle in the corner of the landing beside two others left there and go all the way down to the bar.

The bar is crowded and it takes me forever to get to the front. I order two beers and while I am doing that a girl grabs my arm and for a moment I look for George because I think it's the same girl from upstairs.

The girl says, "You're here with George, aren't you? Did you see where they went?"

I say, "They're up in our room." The bartender brings the beers and I put a bill onto the counter and turn around holding one in each hand. I say, "They're supposed to meet me down here in a few minutes."

She says, "Are both of those for you?"

I say, "They were."

We go outside. The tables are all taken, and so we stand against the wall. I give her one of the beers. She holds out her other hand and says, "I'm Michelle."

I shake her hand and say, "Nice to meet you."

She says, "You're cute."

I say, "So kiss me," because I think it's what George would say.

She says, "I just met you."

I say, "So don't kiss me, then."

She says, "Yeah, you're definitely here with George."

I say, "I'm not sure that's a compliment."

She laughs and sips the beer I gave her. She says, "No, it is. Or maybe it isn't. I don't know yet."

I say, because I can't think of anything else to say, "So you guys are in town for the fiesta?" and regret it even before I'm done saying it because it is a stupid thing to say and because it is exactly what my dad would have said.

She says, "Yep. We were hanging out in Barcelona and we decided to come over and check it out."

And I say, "Oh," and I nod like I understand, like I have any idea what it's like to just be hanging out in Barcelona and decide to come over to check out the fiesta.

She says, "Your friend is funny."

I say, "Oh yeah? Funny how?"

She shrugs and says, "I don't know. He's just funny."

I say, "How did you hook up with him?"

She says, "We went into this bar, just to get out of the sun, and we ended up sitting next to him. Gwen was all pissy because someone had stepped on her foot, and he bet her a kiss that he could make her laugh. He dumped his whole beer onto the head of the guy sitting behind him. We about busted a gut laughing at that. Then the guy started to come after George and so we all ran out."

I say, "That's George all right."

A while later somebody slaps me on the shoulder and it's George and he says, "Why don't you try to make yourself a little harder to find, asshole," and he laughs. He is holding Gwen's hand. He says, "I see you met Gwen's little sister."

I say, "We met."

George says, "Yeah, well, great. Do you have my money?" I hand him the wad and he takes it and says, "Who needs another drink? I'm buying."

Gwen says, "We all do."

George goes inside and when he's gone Gwen turns to Michelle and me and says, "Isn't this great? Don't you just love this town?" She offers me a cigarette and I take one and when she lights it for me I have to try really hard to remember how kids I know look when they're smoking, because I don't. I inhale and I blow smoke like I've been doing it for years and I feel cooler than cool.

Then George comes back with the beers and Gwen gives him a cigarette too, and he looks twice as cool as I do.

He says, "I found the door to the basement of this place. I think we should check it out."

I say, not because I really care but because I haven't had a chance to say anything with a cigarette in my mouth yet, "Why the hell would we want to go down in some dusty old basement?" and I regret saying it right away because it was a stupid thing to say.

Michelle says, "I think it might be kind of cool. These buildings are so old. You never know what you might find."

George says, "Exactly."

Gwen says, "I'll do whatever, as long as I don't end up in jail. Our dad would *kill* us." She laughs and smoke trickles out of her nostrils and I want to be able to do that, but I don't want to try it because I don't want to screw up in front of them.

I say, "Christ, I don't care what we do. Let's go, then," and I stand up to go.

George says, "Calm down, man. Sit down. Finish your beer. Cool it."

I shrug and sit back down, like they're the ones being ridiculous about this. They're not, though, and I know they're not. I can't help it, though. I'm buzzed from the cigarette and the beer and wine and from talking to Michelle. I look at George and George is sitting as cool as anything, like nothing at all can rile him, and for a second I feel like that is the only thing I want to be and the only thing I can't be, no matter how hard I try.

George says, "*Fee-YES-tah. FEE-yes-TAH*," and the girls laugh.

After we finish our beers we go inside. George leads us down a hallway and then opens the door to the closet at the end and in the floor of the closet is a trapdoor. He opens it and tells me to lead the way. I start down and it's dark and I can't find a light switch, so I ask Gwen for her lighter. With the lighter I spot the pull cord and get the lights on. One of the girls, I can't tell which one, calls down the stairs to ask what it looks like and for a second I don't say anything, because they're waiting for me to tell them because only I know.

I say, "Come down."

The girls come down and stand next to me, and Michelle says, "It looks like Grandpa's basement."

Gwen says, "Like, exactly like Grandpa's basement."

I hear the trapdoor close and a second later George is next to us. He says, "Would you look at all this great old stuff?" and I smile because that is totally something his dad would say.

Gwen says, "It looks like a bunch of junk."

Michelle says, "Uh-huh."

George is already rooting through a pile in the corner. He says, "Are you kidding me? You haven't even looked around! You have no idea what you're going to find down here!"

Gwen says, "I'm not going to find anything down here, because I'm going up."

Michelle says, "Me too."

But George doesn't say anything, and I think maybe he didn't hear them because he is making so much noise, going through the pile and the stuff on the shelves. I tell the girls we'll be up in a minute and that we'll meet them in the bar. Then I go over to George and I says, "The girls are leaving."

George says, "So?" and he doesn't look up from what he's doing.

I say, "Anyway, I told them we'd meet them in the bar in a few minutes. What the hell are you doing? They're going to be pissed at us now."

George grins but he still doesn't look up. He says, "Gwen's sister is cute, right?"

I say, "Totally cute."

From the other side of the basement I hear the girls pushing on the trapdoor, but they can't get it open. Then one of them calls for George. I go over and I climb the stairs and I push the door open for them. Michelle kisses me on the top of my head as she climbs past me and says, "Don't be too long."

When they're gone I go back over to George. George is rummaging through another pile, and as I reach him he comes up with a massive circular saw, the kind they cut asphalt with. I say, "What the hell is that doing here?"

George says, "There's a bunch of tools. Some construction guy must keep his equipment down here when he's not using it."

I say, "How lucky for us. In case we want to put an addition on our room, we'll know just where to get the gear for it."

George says, "You know what I want to do with this?" and he's got this tone in his voice that I recognize, the one that I don't trust and don't like anymore.

I say, "No, I don't. I don't think I want to," because all I want to do is go up and be with Michelle, and every second we're away from her it feels like she's slipping away from me.

George says, "I'm going to cut the head off of that fucking Hemingway sculpture."

And I laugh and suddenly I'm not thinking about the girls anymore, because now I'm just thinking about how great George is, and what a character he is, and how glad I am that he's my best friend, and that that's what's important after all. But George isn't laughing, and so I stop laughing. George says, "I am completely, one-hundred-percent dead serious."

I say, "Oh come on. Drop it, man." And then, because he doesn't say anything, I say, "You don't even know if that thing runs. You have no idea how long it's been down here."

So George takes hold of the chord and pulls, and the saw starts up right away. He says something that I can't hear over the sound of the motor, and so I yell for him to repeat what he said. He shuts the saw off and says, "It's happening. Make your peace with it," but he's sort of smiling at the same time.

And I say, "You asshole. You're not going to do it. That's not funny. You can't do that to me. You're going to give me a fucking heart attack. You know we have high cholesterol in my family."

George laughs and suddenly it's all right, like he was joking the whole time, like it's a big joke that I didn't get. He puts the saw down on top of the pile and we go back up to the bar. The girls are there in the crowd, and when we walk over Michelle says, "Let's go down the street and buy a bottle. It's too much work getting drinks from the bar. It's too much waiting. Too many damn tourists."

We leave and walk down the street to a shop that Gwen and Michelle know, and George buys a bottle for each of us. When we step outside Gwen and George put their arms around each other. A group of men come around the corner ahead of us all singing something in Spanish, and George starts singing along, even though he's not singing any of the words, and it's the funniest thing I've ever seen.

Then some time after that the bottles are all empty, and so we go into a bar to get out of the sun and George buys a round of beers to take a break from the wine. We find a booth in the back and sit, and then for a long time there is nothing but Michelle and Michelle's mouth, and the world is the taste of beer and wine and Michelle's tongue and Michelle's tongue is sweet.

After we leave the bar we wander around until dark, drinking more wine. At some point, and somehow, we find out that the girls have nowhere to stay, because then

George is insisting and I am insisting that they stay with us. Then there is a long stretch where I remember nothing, only George holding me by the shoulders and telling me to be cool, be calm, to not blow it, and then we are there together in our room and the girls are there with us, too. Then sleep or something very like it comes overwhelmingly and Michelle lays on top of me with her head resting on my chest and throat in the hollow beneath my chin and the smell of her hair is in my nose and her arms are tucked between us, against my chest and I tell her that I am in love with her, that she is the most incredible person. I stroke her hair and watch her sleep and I can't think of any reason why any of this can't be true. And then I fall asleep.

George wakes me up. The room is still almost dark and he says, "get dressed," and he is up and pulling on his pants. The girls are asleep beside me and George says, "It's past seven. We've got to go."

I get up and get dressed and I while I'm doing that I say, "What about the girls?"

He says, "Let them sleep. We'll be back in an hour anyway. Come on already."

I say, "All right."

We go downstairs and out into the street. The crowd is already gathered in the square, and as we join them someone hands me a bottle and I drink and thank them in Spanish. I feel light and empty and I don't remember most of what I said or did the night before. I hope that it was nothing bad or ridiculous and I think that it probably was, and I remember telling Michelle that I loved her and that she was an incredible person, and I hope and hope and hope that she and everyone else was asleep and nobody heard me.

George says, "You look nervous. You feel all right?"

I say, "I'm still drunk. I have no idea how I look."

George grins. He looks like he is about to say something, but as he opens his mouth the first rocket goes up and we start moving. Then the speed seems to increase from the back in a wave, and I know that the people there have caught sight of the first bulls. George laughs and then people are between us and I can't see him anymore and we are all running. The second rocked goes up and we start really running, and I can hear the yelling from the people around me and the people behind the barricades. I don't see George and I don't see anything but backs and running feet.

Then the man in front of me speeds up, and a space opens in front of me, and the push knocks me forward, and I fall. Someone tries to grab me, but then their hands slip from my sides and I curl up and roll against the barricade and cover my head, so that I can't see and the world is only the thunder of feet and the groaning of the barricades and yelling. Then there is space and I push myself up and I can see the first bull coming fast and he is bigger than anything I have ever seen. Someone pushes me forward and I stumble and I can hear the bull and I feel him behind me and I try to get inside of the crowd but it is moving away from me as fast as I am moving to catch it. Behind the bull there are other bulls and around him there are other bulls. Someone is yelling and then I know that it is me yelling and I know that I am very far away from everything safe and that when I die I will have no one to blame but myself and I hate George very much and passionately because I can't blame him, not fully, not the way I want to, because I want it to be all his fault, and I know that no one will pity me and no one will mourn because it's my own stupid fault and they will be more upset with me than they will be sad that I am gone. And then I see the ring and the gate and I look straight ahead and run harder and I am inside and I dive and hoist myself over the wall and I land on my face and shoulder in the dust and taste blood and breathe dirt. Someone else comes over and lands on me with their knees and they yell at me in Spanish and I roll away, and someone helps me up.

They say, "*¿Cómo está usted?*"

And I say, "Don't worry, I'm fine," and, "I'll be all right, I just need to catch my breath." The words don't make any sense and I know that they can't understand me but I can't do anything to stop myself from saying them. I say, "I thought that bull was going to get me back there, I really did. I have to tell you, I was pretty scared." I say, "I've got to say it, I really really thought I was going to die," and then I start laughing and I wish that I could stop because I can't explain why I am doing it in words that anyone around me will understand. I am worried that they will think that I was afraid and I was afraid but I want to explain about how the bull meant that I did not matter and that I could be wiped out very

easily. But I can't and so I just keep laughing and someone hands me a bottle and I take a long drink and then
cough and say, "*Gracias.*"

The man takes the bottle from me and says, "*De
nada.*"

And I say, because I can't think of anything else to
say, "I guess I'll see you guys later."

I walk down and then out through the gates. The
streets are still crowded but no one is watching the pas-
sageway anymore. I look for George, but I don't see him
anywhere.

When I get back to the room the girls are still asleep,
and I go into the bathroom and take a shower. I wipe the
tears and snot and dust off my face and out of my mouth
and I wash the dirt from my hair. While I'm doing that
the bathroom door opens and one of the girls comes in.
The shower curtain is foggy plastic and I can see her as
she moves into the room, but I can't tell which one it is.
She is wrapped in one of the sheets. She goes to the toi-
let and sits and says, "How did the bulls look?" and I
know that it's Gwen from her voice.

I say, "I didn't really see them," trying to sound like
myself because I think she probably thinks I'm George.

She says, "What? I can't hear you with the water
running."

I say, louder, "I didn't really get a good look at
them."

She says, "Oh." She says, "Michelle and I are going
to the bullfight this afternoon. Are you going?" She

stands up and goes to the sink, and starts splashing water on her face.

I say, "Is George going?"

She says, "I think so." Then she says, "Here. Move over."

She drops the sheet and it lands in a pile on the floor and it lands with no sound against the sound of the running water. Then the curtain comes back and she is in the shower with me, and she pulls the curtain closed, and I study the lines of her back and down and then down her legs down to her ankles. She moves under the water, to the front of the shower, and I slide against the wall. Then she is under the water facing me and the water is running through her hair and she is saying, "I feel so gross. We've been sleeping in tents for the past four days. I thought I was going to crawl out of my skin," and she is running her hands over and over across her head and I am watching her. She looks me over, and I watch her eyes come to rest and she says, "You're sweet, but I really just need a shower."

I say, "Right. Sure. Of course. I mean, of course."

She says, "Are you finished?"

I say, "I don't know. I mean, sure."

And she says, "I'll just be a minute." Then she turns her back to me, and I stand there and I have no idea what to do. I try to think what George would do, but I can't do that. After a while she turns back to me and opens one eye and says, "If you're finished, would you grab me a towel?"

I say, "Sure," and I get out and get her a towel, and while I'm out the water stops. Then she opens the curtain and I watch her wring the water out of her hair and then she takes the towel from me.

She says, "Sorry to intrude."

I say, "Not at all."

She wraps the towel around her and says, "Thanks." Then she steps out of the tub, holding my shoulder so she doesn't slip. When she's out she kisses me on the cheek and says, "Sorry to get your hopes up."

I say, "No problem." I am standing against the wall, covering myself with my hands.

She says, "You're sweet. I can see why Michelle likes you."

She takes the sheet from the floor and leaves the bathroom and closes the door behind her. I stand for a minute, felling the cool from outside from when the door opened. Then I reach over and turn the water back on and I duck underneath it. Outside, above the water noise, I hear the door open and close, and I hear George's voice, but I can't hear what he is saying. I don't want to go see him or talk to him and so I stay under the shower for a long time.

But then George comes in. He stands facing the sink and the mirror and holds his hands up in a gesture of innocence and says, "I'm not looking, I just want to brush my teeth." He wipes the steam from the mirror with his fist. Through the curtain I can see that the back of his shirt is brown with dust and there is blood on his shoulder. He says, "I lost you out there."

I say, "Yeah, I know. The fucking crowd. I got knocked over and they wouldn't even help me up."

He says, "Yeah. I almost thought you didn't make it."

I say, "I almost thought I wasn't going to."

He shakes his head and says, "I can just imagine myself, calling your parents to tell them that you got trampled by bulls." He says this half-forming his words around the toothbrush in his mouth. Then he laughs and spits and says, "If anything happens to you, it better happen to me, too."

I say, "Then we'll both be dead." I say, "That makes me feel a lot better."

I turn off the shower and wrap a towel around my waist. I get out and I move beside him and face the mirror and I start shaving.

George says, "What are you doing, practicing?" because I'm shaving my cheeks, too, and my beard doesn't grow there yet.

I say, "You have to shave all of it. It makes it grow back thicker."

George says, "Where did you hear that?"

I say, "I read it in a magazine or something. Somewhere. I don't know."

He scratches his own beard. The whiskers have come in thick on his chin and around and under his jaw and then sparsely along his cheeks and in front of his ears. It's the same way his father's beard grows. He says, "I'm not going to shave until the *fee-YES-tah* is over."

I say, "Suit yourself."

He says, "That can't be right, can it? I mean, then girls' legs would get super hairy. Where did you read that?"

I say, "I don't know. Maybe I just heard it somewhere." I'm almost finished. I bring the razor up my throat and out to the point of my chin. Then I wash off what's left of the shaving cream. I lean in close to the mirror and pull my upper lip down and look around the bottom of my nose. Then I pull the skin tight across my chin and look for stubble in the seam below my lower lip. Then I turn from side to side, first right, then left, and then I lift my chin and look at my neck and circle my chin back, turning from left to right. I have seen my father do this a thousand times.

George says, "If we're going to get tickets to the bullfight, then we're going to need to get down there. We should have picked them up while we were down at the ring."

I say, "Let's go get tickets and then get breakfast."

George says, "And some more wine. We're out."

"Beer," I say. "I"m too thirsty for wine."

George says, "Beer it is."

We leave the bathroom. Michelle and Gwen are back in bed, under the sheet. I pull pants on under the towel and then I drop the towel and pull on a shirt. Michelle wakes up and rolls over and looks at me.

She says, "Where are you going?"

I say, "We're going to go get tickets to the bullfight. Then we're going to get breakfast."

She closes her eyes and says, "Come get us for breakfast."

I say, "All right."

She says, "Mmmm."

Outside it is crowded behind and in front of the barricades. We walk with the crowd down the center of the street. Everything is too bright and feels too loud and too close and I think that I must be getting sober or at least that I must not be drunk anymore. It feels like many things are happening, but that I can only deal with them one at a time. We try to buy tickets at the booth, but the man tells George that they're sold out. We end up buying a pair from a man who speaks enough English to be confusing. When we get back to the hotel Gwen is up and dressed but Michelle is still curled up under the sheet. We wait out in the hall while she gets dressed and then we all go down for breakfast and afterwards George pays. Outside the restaurant it's bright and sunny but there is thunder somewhere far out and the edge of the sky is gray with rain. We have a few hours until the bullfight. We buy a few bottles of wine and then walk out to the campground and sit among the tents under the trees. Michelle and Gwen know some people from sleeping there the nights before they met us and we sit with them and they drink our wine and we drink theirs. Pretty soon Gwen falls asleep against George's shoulder. I lay back in the grass and listen to George talking to one of the guys Gwen and Michelle introduced us to, and I watch the gray haze move until it is overhead and the sun is a white light somewhere near its center and you can look into it without going blind.

After a while I fall asleep, too. I sleep for a while and then George wakes me up and says that we have to go, that the bullfights are starting. Gwen is opening the last of the wine and she hands it to me and I don't really want it but I drink it anyway and it burns in my throat and then the rest goes down with no feeling at all. We walk back to the town center and then we join the crowd heading toward the ring. George says that we should hurry or we'll miss the beginning and we push through at the gate and sit, waiting. I pass the wine to Michelle and then she passes it past me to George. It's almost gone and I worry that we will need more but I decide that we can get more after, and that if we decide that we can't wait then we can leave in the middle, and that one bullfight is probably a lot like the next.

But then I remember that there is subtlety and art to bullfighting, and I pretend that I understand and appreciate the subtlety and the art, and that it was only the wine and the lack of sleep that made me think that one bullfight was a lot like the next, and that all matadors and all bulls were alike in more ways that they were dissimilar. I tell myself this as the first fight starts and tell myself that I am seeing something about it that no one else is seeing.

But then, before the first fight is even over, I fall asleep. I lay my head on Michelle's lap and I fall asleep. I can feel myself going and when I hear the crowd cheer I tell myself that it is time to sit up, but I don't. And then

I am asleep. And I sleep through the whole thing. I sleep through the whole fucking thing.

I wake up with George shaking me. He says, "Come on. It's time to go."

I say, "What happened? Is it over?"

George says, "Yeah, it's over."

I say, "Why didn't you wake me up?"

Gwen says, "You looked so tired. You looked like you needed the sleep."

Michelle says, "You aren't mad, are you?

I say, "I don't know. I mean, yeah I am. I mean I'm just mad at myself, I guess."

Michelle kisses me and says, "We're going to come back and watch them tomorrow, too. You can see them tomorrow. And besides, you didn't really miss anything. I heard some people talking while I was waiting for the bathroom, and they said that these weren't even very good fights." She says, "Don't be mad."

I say, "I'm not mad."

We follow Gwen and George down the aisle and through the tunnel and out into the street. Above us, the sky is getting darker. Gwen and George and Michelle start talking about the fights, and I feel like the only tourist in the entire town. I walk a few steps behind them with my hands in my pockets and I am angry that I missed it and angry that they didn't wake me up and angry at myself for falling asleep.

Before we get back to the room it starts raining, so we go into a bar and George buys the drinks. After a while of standing a group leaves and we take their table, and I sit with my back against the wall, trying not to listen to George and the girls as they talk about the bullfights. I drink my beer and listen to the rain hitting the roof. I imagine the rain falling on the streets, and imagine the way it must settle the dust inside the ring, and I wonder what they do with the bodies of the bulls that have been killed.

George says that since I'm not doing anything I should go and get more wine, but that I should go down the street to the shop because it will be cheaper and easier to buy it there. He hands me some money and I take it and go. Outside the rain is falling hard in big, heavy drops, and I stay close to the buildings to stay out of it as much as I can.

At the shop I buy a three bottles, but while I'm walking back I lose my grip and all of the bottles slip and break on the street, and all of the wine spills out into the rainwater. And I don't do anything. I just stand there, looking at the broken bottles, and then I hear myself make this noise, kind of like a sob. I sit down on the pavement and I don't care about the rain anymore. I sit and I let it run down through my hair and over my face. I think about Gwen and Michelle and George, and I think that they're all together having fun, and I think that they're sick of me and annoyed at me for sleeping through the bullfights. I think that's why George sent me out into the rain to get the wine, instead of ordering it from the bar. I start thinking about all of the reasons George could be mad at me and be sick of me, and I'm sure that he is, and sure that he would rather be here alone.

But after a while I figure that they're waiting for me, so I go back to the bar. When he sees me George says, "What happened to the wine, man?"

I say, "I tried to carry them all together and they slipped and broke."

He says, "I guess we'll just have to get some more, then."

I say, "I'm not going back out. I'm soaked. Move over and let me in," and I sit down next to him on the bench.

George says, "No use crying over spilled wine."

And I say, "Sure." Then I put my head back against the wall and close my eyes, and I listen to George and the girls and the sounds from the other people in the bar. But it's all only noise, and I don't listen to what any of them are saying. And then I guess I fall all the way asleep, because the next thing I know George is shaking me.

He says, "The rain stopped. We're going to walk back," and I sit up and I feel fully awake and sober for the first time in two days.

We go out into the street together. The cobblestones are slick from the rain and we walk carefully. I put my arm around Michelle's shoulders. Gwen has lit a cigarette, and I reach and take it from between her lips. I drag on it and then I let the smoke out and walk through the cloud and feel it roll up and over my face.

We reach the bar and go up to the room. I go into the bathroom and stand there, looking at my face in the mirror. Then the door opens and Michelle comes in and she closes the door behind her. She puts her arms around my neck. I hold her around the waist and turn her so that her back is to the counter and then I help her up onto the counter. I can hear George and Gwen's voices through the wall and then I hear the bed. Michelle undoes my belt and drops it on the floor. I see myself in the mirror behind her and I close my eyes, and with my eyes closed I feel her and I feel me and then after a while I feel me again and it is only me.

Then we talk for a while. She tells me about her parents and about what she wants to be when she grows up. She tells me about the other countries she and Gwen have been to. She tells me about the book she is reading, about how it has changed her life. She tells me about the guy she was dating before she came on this trip. I tell her about my parents, about the crazy things George and I have done, or about the crazy things that George has done that I have been there for. I tell her what my plans are for the next year and I tell her that I am nervous but that I'm sure it will be all right, that I'm sure everything will work out.

After a while she says, "Do you think it's safe to go out?"

I say, "I don't know."

She says, "I'm going to take a shower."

She takes off her dress and gets behind the curtain, and the water comes on. I stand for a minute, watching my reflection go foggy in the mirror. Then I go out. George is sitting on the edge of the bed, pulling on his shirt. Gwen is under the covers, facing away from me. George looks at me, and he has a look that I know.

He says, "I think I'm going to go for a walk."

I say, "Where?"

He says, "I don't know. Down to the ring maybe," but he says it like he knows just where he's going.

I say, "I'll go with you."

We go downstairs, carrying the last bottle. The bar is crowded and I follow George through and down the hall and then through the trapdoor and down into the basement.

George says, "See if you can find a bag or something. Something big enough to hold the saw." He pulls the chord to turn on the light and starts rummaging around in the junk on the floor.

I say, "What are you going to do with the saw?" even though I have a pretty good idea what he's planning to do.

He says, "Something with handles. Like a duffel bag would be perfect, if you can find one."

I say, "I don't see anything." But then I keep looking because George is still looking, and after a minute I find a brown canvas bag with a big shoulder strap, wadded up on one of the shelves. I say, "Hey, George," and I show him the bag.

He says, "That's perfect," and he comes over and takes it from me and he puts the saw into it and zips it closed.

I say, "Now what?"

George doesn't say anything. I follow him back up the stairs and through the bar and out into the street. I feel nervous and excited and I tell myself that George knows what he's doing and that he needs my help. I want to be part of whatever it is George is about to do, but I am thinking of whatever he is about to do as an intangible and vague act somewhere in the future, something that could just as easily not happen, something so dependent on circumstance that there is no use getting worked up about it until it is already happening.

The streets are empty from the rain. We stay close to the buildings and then we cross the broad open space before the ring and I see the bust glowing dull gold in the splashes of light reflecting off of the puddles. George stops and looks around and then goes across. I watch him go, and then I hurry after him.

He takes the saw out of the bag and pulls the chord, and for a second I hope that the saw won't start, that George will have to give up and that we can go back to the girls and the room where it's safe and nobody can come after us or be upset with us. But then it does, and suddenly there's nothing standing between George and what he's going to do, and it's not just something vague and in the future anymore. I say his name, but I say it low enough that he won't hear me over the saw, low enough that it won't stop him, just loud enough to tell myself later that I tried.

George says, "OK, OK," and even over the sound of the saw I can hear him breathing.

Then he stands up and then there is the loud noise as the saw bites and a line of white and yellow and orange sparks and I watch them hit the pavement and cool against the water and I am hypnotized by them. I can hear George saying, "OK, OK," over and over again to himself over the sound of the saw and I hold myself very still and I strain my ears to hear any sound of someone coming to stop us, even though of course I can hear nothing but the saw and George.

I stand and start pacing. I have no idea what to do. I want to be far away and I want George to be finished and I want to have never come with him. Steam is rising from the blade and the bust where the rain hits it and mixing with the exhaust, and George's face is lit by the sparks.

I have no idea how much time passes, but then he is finished and I hear the saw stop and the head hit the street, and I hear George call my name. I go over and together we roll the head into the bag, and now that it is done and it is all right I wish that I had helped him. So I say, "I'll carry it. I've got it," and I lift the bag and it is heavier than I thought but I don't tell George.

George says, "It's pretty heavy. We can take turns." Beside us the stump is steaming where the rain hits it. George says, "Come on, let's get out of here."

He takes the saw and I take the bag and we cross the open space, and then we are back in the shadows beside the buildings. George tells me to wait and he goes down one of the alleys carrying the saw and then he comes back without it.

I say, "They'll find it."

He says, "Doesn't matter. I wiped the handles, and it'll take them forever to figure out where it came from. We don't even know that whoever that saw belongs to is even around. He probably lives somewhere else part of the time. Why else would he store his equipment there? And besides, we'll be out of here before they even find it. So don't worry."

And I say, "OK," and I try not to worry, because what George says makes sense and anyway it's all I've got to go on.

We carry the bag together, each of us holding one of the straps, until we get back to the hotel. Outside the door George stops me and tells me to act casual and then he takes the bag himself and we go inside.

I watch the people and nobody seems to notice us. George makes for the staircase and I follow after him, but slowly, because I think that it will look less suspicious if it looks like we're not together. Then I go after him, and when I reach him he has the bag on the landing and he says, "You're going to have to help me get this the rest of the way." He is leaning against the wall and breathing heavy and his face is a deep red, deeper than I've ever seen it.

He takes one of the straps and I take the other and we climb the second flight. Halfway up I hear bottles falling and George curses and I see him stumble into the wall. At our floor I pull and George comes up behind me, trembling and gritting his teeth. He stops and puts his hands on his knees and says, "Fuck it, let's just drag it the rest of the way," and together we drag it down the hall to our room. Halfway down he lets go and when I reach the door I look back and see him leaning against the wall with his eyes closed. Without looking he says, "I'm fine. Just give me a minute. I'm all right."

I say, "We didn't talk about the girls."

George says, without opening his eyes, "What about them?"

I say, "You know. I mean, if we can trust them or not."

George pushes off the wall and comes toward me. He says, "The girls are cool. Don't worry about the girls."

I open the door and drag the bag into the room. Then I fall onto the bed and I lay there with my eyes closed and catch my breath. George come in and lays down next to me, and we don't say anything for what feels like a very long time. Then after a while he starts to laugh, and I start laughing, too. I feel sick from being winded and my chest and my stomach hurt. George gets up and he rolls the head out of the bag, and we sit there just looking at it for a while.

I say, "Where are the girls?"

George says, "I don't know. Don't worry. They probably just got hungry or something."

I say, "I need a drink."

George says, "Me too."

But then neither of us gets up. We stay there, staring at the head. A while later the girls come in. Gwen comes in first. She looks at us sitting on the bed and I watch her look from us to the head on the floor and then Michelle comes in after her and Michelle closes the door.

Gwen says, "Holy shit." She looks at the head and then at us and says, "Holy shit," again, and looks back at the head. She says, "Holy shit you guys. I mean, holy shit," and George laughs and she looks at him and says, "What the hell? I mean... What the hell?"

Michelle says, "What?" because from where she's standing she can't see. I lay back on the bed and George does the same and I stare at the ceiling and I smile because I hear Michelle saying, "Jesus Christ, you guys. Jesus."

And then Michelle is over me and her hair is wet and smells good from the rain as it hangs in my face and she kisses me and for a long time there is nothing else and nothing else matters.

And then George is saying "We've got to go, man. Then run starts in twenty minutes."

I say, "I'm staying here. You run. I'm going to stay here."

George says, "Come on, man. You've got to come. Come on. I'm not going to go do it by myself. Get up, man."

I say, "All right, just shut up already, would you?" and I sit up.

George says, "Attaboy."

We zip the head into the bag and then roll it into the bathroom and close the door. The girls tell us that they'll see us when we get back. George tells me that we have to hurry and so we go down and through the bar and out into the street.

The sun is coming up and the sky is clearing but the street is still wet. We go down to the square and we stand outside the crowd and then we stand at the edge of the crowd and then we are part of the crowd. We wait for a long time, and I think maybe they already saw the statue, maybe the rocket is never going to go up, maybe they cancelled the fiesta. But then the first rocket goes up and we all start moving, and the second rocket goes up and the crowd picks up speed as we move into the narrow corridor between the barricades. Then the bullring is up ahead and I do not look to where I know the pedestal is and then we are under the corridor and then we are in and we move out of the ring with the damp brown dirt caked to our shoes and I stick with George as we climb up into the seats and watch the last of the runners coming in. Then the bulls come, and George laughs, and we leave.

Outside the ring there is a crowd gathered around the pedestal. People are shouting in Spanish then I hear the sirens coming from far away and I listen as they get closer and then the crowd is pushed back and there is voice on a loudspeaker but the voice is speaking in Spanish, and I feel nauseas and for a moment I think that I'm going to be sick. I hear George asking people what happened, but I think that he is asking too many people and he is asking over and over.

I say, "George, we really ought to get back, don't you think?"

George says, "Does anyone know what happened? Did anyone see what happened?" and he looks at me like I need to watch myself, like I'm the one making the scene.

I say, "I'm going back to the room. You stay and find out what happened," and I say this last part extra loud so that George knows that everyone around us thinks that we don't know what happened. Then I start back up towards the room. But after a few steps George catches up with me and puts his arm around my shoulders.

He says, "Ok, I think we've got them fooled."

And I stop walking and I face him and I say, "You're a fucking idiot. You think we've got them fooled? What the hell are you talking about? This is the goddamned dumbest thing that you have ever thought of doing, bar none. Oh Jesus Christ. Jesus George we are so fucked." All of a sudden I feel like if I keep talking I'm going to start crying, so I stop. George just looks at me, and after a minute I shake my head and I start back again. After a dozen steps I turn around and George is still standing there, watching me go.

He says, "You're an asshole. I didn't ask you to come with me. I don't know why I brought you on this trip in the first place."

And I say, "I wish you hadn't."

Then I turn around and I start walking again, and I don't look back anymore.

The bar isn't very crowded. I think that it's probably because most of the people are still down at the ring, or still working their way back. I sit at the bar and have a beer and then I have another. I think of what will happen when they find us and for a while it seems like I am thinking about it happening to other people and none of it seems too bad and none of it seems to have anything to do with George and me. Then I start thinking about not going home and not seeing my parents and I realize that it is us and not someone else and I start to wish very much that we hadn't done it. I think that if we turn ourselves in they will go easy on us. I think the statue can be fixed. I think a lot of stupid things.

Then George comes in. I don't see him until he sits down at the bar next to me. He orders a beer and thanks the bartender in Spanish, and when the beer comes he drinks half of it in one swallow.

I say, "So did you find anything out?"

He says, "No."

I say, "You think they're going to start looking in town?"

George snorts and he says, without looking at me, "How should I know what they're going to do?" He finishes the beer in another long swallow and then gets up and heads for the stairs.

I leave what's left of my beer and go up after him. We go down the hall together and we go into the room one right after the other, and so we see at the same time that all of our stuff has been pulled out of our bags and is scattered around the room, and that the girls are gone.

George walks in a circle around the bed, looking at the floor. Then he grabs a pair of pants off the bed and start checking the pockets. He says, "Oh fuck," and he starts checking the pockets in another pair. Then he throws the pants down and he starts pushing the blanket back and forth and looking under it. And he is saying, "Oh fuck. Oh Jesus. Oh fuck," and his voice sounds distant and then tight like I have never heard it. Then he picks up another pair of pants and checks the pockets. Then he checks another pair. Then he drops down and I hear him rifling around under the bed and I can hear his voice muffled through the mattress saying, "Oh fuck, oh fuck, oh fuck." He starts beating the mattress with his fist and then he stands and picks up one side and tries to throw it. But it only goes up and then comes back down, in more or less the same place.

And I say, just because there's nothing else to say, even though I already know, "What?"

And George says, "It's gone, man. The money is gone," and he says it with his head hanging down and his arms covering his face so that I can barely understand him.

I say, "Maybe they just went out to get some wine or something. You know? Maybe they just went out for a minute. They're probably coming back."

George looks up, and his face is red and there are tears in his eyes. He says, "Look around, man. Think about it. They've been *planning* this."

I say, "Come on, man," and I go over and I sit down on the edge of the bed next to him. I say, "That's crazy. That doesn't seem like something they would do, does it? I bet they're just out getting some wine or something," and as I say it I'm looking at the mess on the floor, and thinking that what I am saying sounds pretty unlikely.

George says, "Don't you get it? There is no "seems like" something they would do. You don't know what they would do because you don't *know them*. They were *playing* us. Jesus *Christ*," and he isn't even crying anymore, because now he's only angry.

I say, "That's crazy man. That's. I don't know. Things like that don't happen in real life, George."

George says, "Then where's the money? Why is our shit all over the floor?"

I look at my stuff all scattered around, and I think that he's probably right. Still, I think, it doesn't seem like something Michelle would do. I think about Michelle telling me all about her parents and the town she's from. Then I think, You're a fucking idiot. How can you still be thinking like that? And then I think, You've got to hand it to them. And so I say, "All right. All right. Lets just calm down. What do you want to do?"

George is looking at the floor and for a minute I wait for him to answer and then when he doesn't answer I think maybe he isn't going to. Then after a while he says, "Lets go downstairs and have a drink. I think I just need a drink."

I say, "All right."

We go back down to the bar. The bar is more crowded, now. George orders us a couple drinks. He asks the bartender if he has seen the girls, if he saw them leave, but the bartender only shrugs. We find an empty table and sit and while we are sitting a lot more people come in.

I feel like the new people are looking at us, and so I keep looking at my drink. I can hear people talking around us but I am not paying attention. I sit and drink my drink and try to think of what we can do. I think if we can get rid of the head and get out of town we will be all right, and that no one knows that George and I were involved except the girls. I think that maybe we can get the head into one of our backpacks and we can leave other things if we need to but that the head will fit in the bag itself and then we can carry it and it will look just like any other tourist with a backpack and no one will think twice if they see us.

After a while I say, "So what do you want to do?"

George says, "I don't know," and he says it like he's mad at me for asking.

I say, "I mean, we should probably go to the police, right? About the girls?"

George says, "So they can come inspect the scene of the crime? And maybe they won't notice the huge fucking piece of evidence in the middle of the floor?"

I say, "Maybe it wouldn't be so bad."

And George says, "What?"

I say, "Telling the police. Think about it. Maybe we're making a bigger thing of this than it really is. I mean, to these people we're just a couple of stupid drunk American kids. Maybe they'll think of it as a prank, you know? I bet they can weld the head back on, and you and me will get transferred to some court in the U.S., and they'll give us community service or something. You know? Maybe it's not that big a deal."

George says, "Yeah, yeah, and maybe it's a huge deal. Maybe it's the biggest deal these people have ever seen, and everyone who ever got pissed at an American for coming into town for the bullfights and getting drunk and throwing up in the street is going to see this as their chance to get back at all Americans. Maybe they make an example of us. Maybe they do that. Did you think about that? Huh? I'm not going to talk to the police to try to find out which one it is."

I say, "So what are we going to do," and it is less of a question at this point than it was when I asked the first time.

George says, "I don't know."

I say, "Fine." I say, "If you're not going to do anything about it then I am."

I get up and I cross the bar and go upstairs. On the stairs I look back and see that George is following me and I wait for him on the landing. Then we go up to the room. I empty out what's left in my pack, and then I lay the backpack flat on the ground and I roll the head towards it. Then I hold the top of the backpack open and try to roll the head in. I hold the top open with one hand and try to push the head in with the other. I look at George but George doesn't move to help me. Then I move so that I am holding the top open with both hands and pushing the head with my feet. The head goes in and I stand and lift the bag and the head slides down to the bottom. Then I start stuffing clothes in on top of it and into the sleeping bag compartment underneath it. While I am doing this George sits on the edge of the bed and watches me.

I say, "You could help me, you know."

George says, "You're doing just fine on your own."

I say, "You don't have to be such an asshole."

George shrugs and says, "I'm an asshole. Sorry."

I'm holding a handful of clothes that won't fit because the head doesn't leave room for them. I say, "Can you pack these, please? They won't fit."

George shrugs and says, "They're your clothes. If you can't fit them then that's your problem."

I throw them at him and I say, "Fuck you George. I cannot believe you're doing this right now. You're acting like a child."

He shrugs again and says, "I'm being completely rational. You can tell, because I'm not helping you. If I was helping you, then you would know that I was being completely *ir*rational. What's the plan? We're going to just walk out of town with the head in a backpack? That's laughable, man."

I say, "Have you got a better idea?" He looks at me for a minute, then looks away, then shrugs again. I say, "If you don't have a better idea, then help me with this one. The police are going to find the saw and sooner or later they're going to figure out where it came from. When they do they're going to start searching this place, and they're going to find the head. When they do that they're going to find us. And even if by some miracle we could hide it, we have the bill to pay and we don't have any money." I count these off on my fingers. I say, "Now to me, running from our problems seems like a pretty good option right now. Unless you've got something better."

George doesn't move for a minute. Then he slides off the bed and starts picking up the clothes I threw at him.

After a couple of minutes we have everything packed. Then George helps me get my backpack up onto the bed and then I squat down and put my arms through the straps and buckle the belt around my waist and when I stand up the backpack is heavy but it's manageable. We go out into the hall and George says, "They're going to see us leaving."

I say, "We have to stay along the back wall. There was a pretty big crowd in the bar. They won't see us," and I'm breathing hard already.

George says, "OK."

We go down to the bar. The room is even more crowded now, and we have to push our way through. I don't look towards the other side of the room where I know the bartender is standing. I keep moving and then I am to the door and then I am through the door and then I am out in the street and I take off and George is ahead of me and I can't tell if there are others chasing us. I jog maybe thirty yards, and then I have to stop and catch my breath. George comes back and waits with me and we lean against the wall of the nearest building and I watch the bar door for the bartender. But nobody comes out, and after a while we start moving again.

We walk out of town and down to the train station. It is a long walk and it takes a long time and it feels like it takes an even longer time than it actually does. I feel sick to my stomach and I try not to think about it. We walk down beside the tracks, far out from the station to the end where the cargo cars are coupled, and when no one is looking we shove my backpack through an open door and George does the same with his and then we climb up and sit there, breathing heavy in the hot dark.

After a long time the train starts. I'm half-asleep and sick and starting to get hung-over, with nothing to drink since the morning. I curl up against the wall and I try to sleep but now the motion of the train is too violent. Eventually I get used to it, though, and I fall asleep. When I wake up it is dark and I'm thirsty and I say, "George, come help me with this." I unpack my bag and turn it over, and the head slides out. We push it to the edge and then we give a big push with our feet and it just drops off and is gone, like it was never even there. George sits looking after it for a while, and then he lays back on the floor. I can't think of anything to say, so I put everything back into my backpack and then I go back to sleep against the wall.

I wake up when the train starts to slow. It's getting light outside, and I can see George up and pulling on his backpack. I stand and pull my backpack on, too, and then George looks out and jumps down and I do, too. We run along the gravel beside the tracks and then push through a stand of trees and climb a fence and we drop down on the other side, into a neighborhood. We walk along the street for a while, and then we start passing shops and restaurants and George says we should probably change out of these clothes and so we find a café and change in the bathroom and I wash my face in the sink. Then I go out and George orders two waters and we sit by the window and drink them and I say, "Do you want to call or do you want me to?"

George says, "It doesn't matter. It's going to be the same either way."

I say, "I'll call."

I get up and I go into the back by the bathrooms where there's a telephone. I dial my parents' phone number and I wait for a long time, and then my mother answers and says my name.

I say, "Hi mom. How did you know it was me?"

She says, "It's two in the morning, honey. Are you all right? What happened? Are you both all right?"

I say, "We're both fine."

My mother says, "Oh thank God," and the relief in her voice makes me want to cry.

I say, "Mom, George got robbed. These people, they jumped us, and George had all of his money on him and the guys took it. We don't have any money."

My mother says, "He was carrying it all in cash? Oh sweetie, you never travel with cash. Things like that happen. Oh good grief. Did you go to the police?"

I say, "Well, no, see, the thing is that we were just about to catch this train, and since we didn't have any more money we figured that if we missed our train we wouldn't be able to catch another one because we had already bought our tickets and so we had to get on the train right away and we didn't have time to go to the police."

My father's voice cuts in on the other extension. He says, "What happened?"

My mother says, "The boys got mugged."

My father says, "You got mugged?"

I say, "Yeah. These guys, they took all of George's money."

My father says, "That's terrible. Are you all right?"

I say, "Yeah, I was just telling mom, I'm fine. We're both fine."

My father says, "That's terrible, just terrible. I told you, you have to be careful over there. I did tell you. Don't say I didn't warn you."

My mother says, "Leave him alone."

My father says, "I'm just saying, I warned him about things like this."

My mother says, "Where are you, dear? We can Western Union you some money."

I say, "Uh. Hold on." I set the phone down and I run out front and I say, "They want to send us some money Western Union, but they need to know where we are. Where are we?"

George says, "We're in Paris."

I say, "Thanks." I go back to the phone and I say, "Mom? Mom, we're in Paris."

She says, "Really? Paris?"

My dad says, "City of lights."

My mom says, "I always wanted to go to Paris. What's it like?"

I say, "It's wonderful. About the money?"

My father says, "How much do you need?"

I say, "Our return tickets aren't for a week yet."

He says, "Will a couple thousand do?"

I say, "Yeah, that would be great. Sure, yeah, perfect."

He says, "Wonderful. I'll send when I go into work in the morning. That's in six hours. Will you be all right until then?"

I say, "Sure." I say, "We'll be fine."

He says, "OK. Have fun and be safe, all right?"

I say, "Sure, dad."

My mom says, "I love you. Please please please be careful."

I say, "I will."

She says, "It makes me so mad, just thinking about it. Will you call the police, now that you're where you were going? Will you call them and report the theft? Listen. That way at least, are you listening? That way at least the police will have a description on file. You two are lucky that you didn't get hurt. You did the right thing, giving them your money. Money you can always get more of. There's only one of you."

I say, "Right. Got it, mom."

She says, "Please be careful. I love you. Take lots of pictures. I want to see what Paris looks like, ok? Love you," and she makes a kissing sound into the phone.

I say, "Ok. I've got to go, mom. I'll talk to you later." Then I hang up. I go back to the table, and George is still staring out the window. I say, "My parents are sending us some money."

He says, "How much?"

I say, "A couple thousand dollars."

He nods without looking at me and says, "Thanks for doing that. I just really don't feel like I can talk to my parents right now. I just... I just don't have the energy for another lecture."

I say, "I understand."

He says, "What did you tell them?"

I say, "I told them we got mugged."

He says, "I kind of figured." Then he sighs and looks like he is going to say something, but then he doesn't. He just sits there, staring out the window into the street.

We sit in the café for a while, then we wander around until we think the money has arrived. Then we go and get the money. It's all there. I fold the bills into my pocket and then we go and eat lunch. George orders us beers with lunch but I only drink half of mine. After lunch we find a hotel room and I go into the bathroom and I take a shower and I wash all of the dirt and sweat out of my hair and then I put on my last clean set of clothes. When I come out George is asleep on the bed, so I ride the elevator down to the bar and I order a drink and I sit looking at it for a while. Then George comes in and slaps me on the back and sits down at the bar beside me. The bartender comes over and George orders one of whatever I'm having and the bartender says then I will bring you nothing, and George laughs and slaps me on the back again and points at my drink and says well then I'll have one of those, and the bartender nods and goes away.

George says, "What do you want to do today?"

I say, "I don't care."

George says, "Come on. Don't be like that. You should be feeling good right now."

I say, "Well I don't. I don't feel good, George. I don't feel good at all."

The bartender brings George's drink and he sips it and says, "Well I feel good. I feel good."

I say, "I'm sure you do."

I feel him wanting to say something else, but he doesn't. We don't talk anymore, and when his drink is finished he gets up and slaps me on the back again, and leaves. I don't watch him go and I think I probably should, so that I know whether he's back in the room or out somewhere, but then I think that it doesn't matter. I finish my drink, and then have a couple more. I take out my parents' money to pay for the drinks and it unfolds on the bar and I stare at it for a while. Then the bartender comes and I pay and I fold the bills and stuff them back into my pocket.

I leave the bar, and the elevator comes and carries me up. The elevator is glass and as it rises above the lobby I see George coming across the floor and George sees me. He watches me as I go up and I watch him get smaller and for a moment I am glad that he is not with me, glad that I am leaving him behind, glad that he is not there. I want to throw something and I want to watch it fall and when it hits I want it to bury him into the earth so that there is no trace of his ever having been. I want everything I was dumb enough to believe and listen to rewound and erased and I want to be home and in my father's house and I want never again to stray. But instead I just ride the elevator, and when the door opens I step off onto our floor. The room is cool and from the street outside there is no sound. I stand staring out the window, looking out across the city, and when George comes in I don't turn around.

He says, "There are some American girls down in the lobby." He says, "I told them about you." He says, "I said we'd buy them a drink, but you've got all of our money." He says, "Come on."

I follow him out, and we ride down together. As we cross the lobby I see the girls, the ones he was telling me about, standing by the desk. They are blonde and young and beautiful, and I want to collapse into their arms and forget myself and just be blank and empty inside. I want to sleep for a thousand years. But I don't. I shake their hands as George says their names. Then we leave the hotel together. Outside the sun is bright and the sky is clear, and we set off walking with no destination in mind.

The Frost Came Early

The frost came early, and all of the flowers died. The gardeners were out in the morning, and you could hear them cursing in Spanish. Nobody thought that the frost would come and so no one had bothered to cover the flowers. By eleven o'clock it was warm again, and you could stand on your balcony without shivering and watch the gardeners replanting the beds. I did that for a while and when I went in I left the door open and sat on the bed, listening to them. I don't speak Spanish, but I enjoyed listening to them.

When I got tired of that I got dressed and then went downstairs. Some of the other kids were already in the café, drinking coffee. I didn't feel much like sitting with them, but there wasn't really any way not to. I sat down and ordered coffee, too. I didn't feel much like drinking it, but it came and so I did. Everyone looked tired and sick and when the food came no one ate very much. They just drank their coffee. There were televisions all around the café, and everyone watched one. All of the televisions showed the same news. I don't care about the news, but I watched anyway. There was nothing else to do.

After we finished our coffee two of them when to play tennis, and I said I would go with them. I don't play tennis, so I sat and watched them play. One of my favorite things is to close my eyes during a volley and listen to the sound the ball makes on the rackets. It's something I used to do when I was a child and my parents played. It's difficult to explain. But anyway, when the game was over we all walked back together. The two I was with talked, but I didn't listen to what they were saying. I don't listen much to people that I'm with. I listen to plenty, but I don't listen much to that.

When we got back everyone we knew was gone from the café. I went back up to my room and listened to the gardeners working outside. It made me happy that all of the flowers the frost had killed were being removed and new ones put in their place. I ordered lunch and when it came I took it out onto the balcony so I could watch the gardeners working.

Then the telephone started ringing. The telephone was in the room, next to the bed. I listened to it ringing. Then after a while it stopped. When it stopped I went back to eating. I hadn't noticed it, but while the phone was ringing I had mashed my fingers right through my sandwich. After I saw that I wasn't very hungry anymore.

When I went back inside the light was blinking on the telephone that meant that I had a message. I couldn't remember how to retrieve a message on the hotel phones. I tried to remember for a while, and then I called the front desk. They said that they could play the message for me. So then I listened to the message. It was from my Mother. She wanted to make sure that I was having a good time. I said that I was, but then it kept playing and I remembered that it was just a message.

After that it was time for me to take my pill. I'm supposed to take my pills when I eat, but I hadn't thought of it until after I was finished. I had them in my shaving kit. I went into the bathroom to get them and because that's where the faucet and the glasses were. One whole wall of the bathroom was a mirror, and so it was impossible not to see my reflection. It's always strange to see my reflection. All of the boys went to the same barber and he gave them all the same haircut. It's a very neat haircut and it looked the same on everyone. There's only one boy I ever knew who it looked strange on. It looked strange on him because it didn't fit his personality. It looked fine on everyone else. It only looked strange on me because I wasn't used to it. From the outside you couldn't tell that it was strange. After I took my pill I went back out onto the balcony, but the workers were gone. I guess they were eating lunch. With the workers gone there wasn't much of anything to listen to.

The Proctor met us in the café at dinner. He introduced himself to each of us and then sat down. You could tell right away that some of the kids didn't like him. I didn't have much of a feeling about him, one way or the other. He was just the Proctor. After he sat down he went over the rules again. I already knew the rules, but I listened to them anyway. You couldn't do anything else. But while he was going over the rules our food came and I started eating. I wasn't trying to be rude, I was just hungry and so I started eating. But the Proctor seemed to take it that I was being rude. Anyway, at least that's what some of the others said afterward. I didn't notice it. When he was done going over the rules he led everyone in Bless Us O Lord. He went into it without any warning, and so when he started I had food in my mouth. You're supposed to say it before every meal, but

I usually forget. It doesn't matter that I forget, because if someone really wants you to say it they make sure everyone says it together. In the dining hall the Priest stands up before every meal and makes everyone say it. You never have to remember, because the Priest is always there.

After the Proctor finished Bless Us O Lord he said he would see us in the morning and he left. He was going to go eat in his room. Once he was gone the others started making jokes about him. Then they told me how classic it was, that I had started eating right in the middle of his speech. I tried to tell them that I hadn't meant it to be classic, that I was just hungry. They didn't care, though. After dinner I went back to my room to pack everything and take my pill. I also called the front desk, and asked them to wake me up in the morning. I was happy that I had remembered. But the person at the front desk said that a wake up call had already been arranged for all of the boys by the Proctor. After that there was nothing else to do. I got undressed and got into bed. It wasn't very late, but there was nothing else to do.

Pretty soon I got up and went to sit out on the balcony. The gardeners were back working, and so I listened to them. They were pulling big sheets of plastic over the flower beds, to protect the new flowers from the frost. I thought how nice it would be, to be one of those flowers. I thought that maybe it would be nice to tend to flowers, too. I tried to imagine what it would be like to be one of the gardeners. I'm not very good at imagining things.

Then, all of a sudden, I remembered that I hadn't called my Mother back. It was too late by then. I knew that I would hear about it the next time we spoke. Whenever she gets upset my Mother can hardly function. She goes to bed and can hardly stand to see anyone. My Father has to take care of her. She's upset a lot of the time. I felt sorry, because I knew my not having called would make her upset and so it would make trouble for him. There wasn't anything to do about it, though.

After I realized there wasn't anything to do about it I tried to relax. I hadn't noticed that I was doing it, but while I was thinking about my Parents I had taken big handfuls of my robe and bunched them together. After I noticed I let them go, but I still didn't feel very relaxed. So instead I tried to imagine being a gardener. I'm not very good at imagining things, and pretty soon I gave up. Then I thought about being a flower, underneath a big sheet of plastic protected from the frost. For some reason it was easier to imagine that. Imagining that, I felt relaxed. I went back inside and got into bed. Once I was in bed, it was easy to fall asleep.

Then the phone woke me up. I don't dream anymore, since I started taking the pills. I never dreamed very much that I could remember, but now with the pills I don't dream at all. That's why it seemed like I fell asleep and the phone woke me up, one right after the other. I answered the phone just to make sure that it wasn't my Mother trying to call again before I left. But it wasn't my Mother, it was the front desk calling to wake me up. I took a shower and got dressed, and then I took one of my pills from the shaving kit and put it in my pocket. I had to pack up my shaving kit, and I had to take one of the pills with breakfast. When that was done I took everything downstairs. All of the other kids were already there. The Proctor was pacing around by the door. He kept checking his watch. None of the others spoke or moved very much. They all had that same sick look they'd had the last morning at breakfast. I had been hoping that we would have breakfast before we left. I was hungry, and I had to take my pill. But then two more boys came in and the Proctor told everyone to get on the bus. There was a bus waiting right outside. I tried to look and see the flowers from my seat, but I couldn't. I should have looked to see if there was any frost on the ground, but I didn't think to do it when I stepped outside, and from inside the bus you couldn't really tell.

It took a long time to get to the marina. I had a book I had been reading. It was a book about oceanography. My Parents had given it to me. It was a very thorough book. I used to read more fiction. Now it doesn't interest me. English used to be my best class. Now it doesn't seem very interesting. It just seems kind of silly, arguing over who meant what. There's no way to ever know.

When we got to the boat the Proctor made us all stand in a line along the edge of the dock with our bags next to us. Everyone was allowed one duffel and one personal bag. A few of the boys had more than they were allowed, and the Proctor made them repack. He made them do it right there on the dock. Then he put the bags with the things they were leaving back on the bus. I was happy that I had packed the right number of things. It would have been horrible, to have all of my things spread out over the dock for everyone to see. I was glad that my bags were closed, that nobody could see inside of them.

When everyone was finished repacking and the extra bags had been put back on the bus we all got onboard the boat. They took us to our quarters right away. It was one big room with bunk beds. At School my parents had arranged it so I had my own room, but on the boat no one had their own room. Even the Proctor slept in the same room with us. He went around, telling each boy which bunk was his. This was so we would know where to leave our bags. Then we all went back up on deck.

The Captain was waiting for us on deck. The Proctor told us to listen to the Captain and then the Captain started talking. The Captain had a very loud voice. He was talking about the rules onboard the ship. Then he started talking about the jobs everyone would have. Then he told us about what time we would be eating meals and going to sleep. Then he told us the places on the boat we had no business being. After that he welcomed us aboard. While the Captain was talking I wasn't really listening, so after he was finished I wasn't sure if there was something I was supposed to do, something he had told everyone that I hadn't heard. I wondered because everyone else headed back below decks like they had somewhere to go and all knew something that I didn't. I had this feeling I used to get a lot, before I started taking the pills. It was right behind my belly button and it felt like my insides were being squeezed together. It didn't hurt. I'm not describing it right. But then I followed them and it turned out they were just going back to the bunks to put their things away. I put my things away, too. There were gray metal lockers between all the beds. There was one for each bunk, and there was only room for the things we were allowed to bring. When I saw that I understood why the Proctor had made the boys unpack on the dock. There was really nothing else to do. The extra things they brought wouldn't have fit.

I wasn't sure if the Captain had said something I needed to hear because while he was talking I was thinking about Oysters. I was reading about them in the book my Parents gave me, and I was still thinking about them. The Oyster is a bivalve mollusk which eats by filtering Plankton though its gills. The only other thing it does is hold its shell closed. Not all Oysters produce pearls. In fact, the ones that produce pearls aren't even of the same family as common Oysters. Most Oysters don't do anything. They just lay at the bottom of the ocean, eating Plankton. That is their whole life. There were a lot of pictures of them in the book I had.

After everyone put their things away we went up to the mess hall. The mess hall was a lot bigger than I thought it would be. All of the crew members were already eating. There were two tables near the wall that the others had left empty. The Proctor told us all to sit down. Then he sent us up to the food line, two at a time. He waited until the two ahead were halfway through before sending the next two. Some of the boys started to complain because it didn't make much sense. The Proctor didn't care, though. He sent us up two at a time until we were all through. Then he had us all say Bless Us O Lord. I was one of the last to go through the line, and so I hadn't started eating yet. Otherwise, I'm sure I would have.

While I was in line getting food I remembered that I hadn't called my Mother. I thought that it would be all right, because she would call the School and the School would tell her that everyone got on the boat fine. I was certain that the Proctor had to report back. Still, I was sorry I hadn't called. I knew that she would worry. I guess it didn't matter, because I knew she would worry all the same, whether I called or not. Still, I wished that I had called.

I was very hungry, but after I got my food I couldn't eat. The boat was still tied up at the dock, but if you paid attention you could feel it moving. The movement came from the water. They had warned us about it back at School. There were pills you could buy for the motion sickness. They'd even had them on sale at the School bookstore. I hadn't bought any. I wished that I had. I knew I could have asked one of the other boys, because I lot of them had bought the motion sickness pills. I also knew that I could ask the Proctor. I was sure that he had some. But I didn't feel like doing either of those things. I felt like going and standing on solid ground. I took my tray and went up on deck. The ramp was still connected, and I walked off and stood on the dock. Standing on the dock I felt much better. I sat down and started eating. Then, someone called my name. Then the Proctor came down the ramp. I stood up, because I thought he was going to hit me. I don't know why I thought that, because I knew that he couldn't. The School would have fired him. He came over and knocked the tray out of my hands. He asked me what the hell I thought I was doing. I told him that I was feeling sick and that I came out to stand on solid ground. He said that wasn't the way it worked. Then he grabbed my arm and started pulling me back up the ramp. When we were back on the boat he told me to stay where I was. Then he went back down the ramp and picked up the tray. It was funny watching him do it, but I didn't laugh because my arm hurt from where he had been holding me. Then he came back onboard and told me to go back to my bunk. So I went back below deck. He walked behind me all the way to the bunk room.

Once I was back in my bunk I realized I hadn't taken my pill. I forgot that I had one in my pocket. I started looking around in my locker for them. I was nervous, because I thought maybe the Proctor wanted me to stay in bed, and would hear me moving around. But then I found my pills and I took one. I took it without any water. When I first started taking them I couldn't hardly get them down. Now it's not very hard to take them without water. After I took it I started reading my oceanography book. I couldn't concentrate though, because I was still hungry. I just lay on my stomach, looking around the room. All the bunks looked the same, and they all had the same kind of duffel bag hanging from the posts. Seeing that made me think about the haircut that all the boys had. Then I started thinking about the one boy who the haircut had looked strange on. I wondered where he was. The School is very hard to get into, because they have such a long tradition. They're always talking about their tradition, about how the tradition makes the School better than other Schools. Whenever they talk about the tradition, what they're really talking about is the teaching method they use. The method is named after one of the teachers who developed it. When you first apply they give you a lot of information about how terrific the method is, and how they're the only School in the country teaching the authentic version. Then, at the end of all of this literature about it, they have a clause about what if the method doesn't work for you. The clause says that "certain individuals" don't learn well with the method approach. Every boy who comes to the School reads that clause, and when a boy doesn't understand something in class everyone else starts calling him a "certain individual." At the School, "certain individual" means stupid. But that was this kid, the kid who didn't look right with the haircut. He was a certain individual. He didn't last a semester.

After a while all of the boys came back. I was happy, because I remembered how they'd all said it was classic when I started eating while the Proctor was talking, and I thought maybe they would say it was classic, that I had gone back onshore. But none of them seemed very interested. They all sat in a cluster around somebody's bunk, talking. After a while I went back to reading my book. I was reading a very interesting thing about how a reef forms over thousands and thousands of years.

Then, I don't know why, I had this really funny idea. I thought that I would like to swim around the boat. But I didn't get up to do it or anything. I just stayed in my bunk. After a while I must have fallen asleep, because I woke up when the Proctor came in. He came in telling everyone to get in bed. Then he said that lights out was in five minutes. He had the Captain with him. The Captain welcomed everyone onboard again, and then told everyone to sleep well because we were going to launch in the morning. Then the Captain went out, and everyone started getting in bed.

I tried to read some more, but it was no good. I can't read when I know they're going to shut the lights off at any second. Or when my train is pulling into the station soon or when the plane I'm on is going to land. Things like that. I read, but I don't remember any of it afterwards. Anyway pretty soon they shut off the lights. There was a lot of noise for a while and then the others started to fall asleep and it was quiet. I could hear the water against the sides of the boat. It had been there all along, but now it was the only thing to listen to. I thought about the workers replanting the beds at the hotel. I wondered if there was going to be frost again, and would they cover the flowers, or would they just hope for the best. I figured that they wouldn't just hope for the best, but I didn't know. It was too early for frost, so maybe it wouldn't come again for a while. And then I thought what if it did, and they came out in the morning and all of the new flowers had died. It really bothered me. It was the sort of thing that bothered me, that they always told me not to be bothered by. The flowers are just one example. There have been a million things my Parents have told me to just let go. But I can't. For some reason, I can't let go of them. I stay up at night, thinking about them. Laying awake on the boat, I was sad that the new flowers might get killed by the frost. I don't know why. It doesn't make any sense.

I woke up because the boat was making a horrible noise. Everybody else was up, too. Somebody asked the Proctor what it was. But the Proctor didn't have to answer, because one of the other boys did. It was the engines. It was pretty obvious, if you thought about it. I was glad I hadn't asked what the noise was.

We all got dressed and went up on deck. We were only a little way off, but I was surprised how fast the dock was moving away. Whenever you see a big ship you always think it's moving slowly, because you only see it out in the water where there's nothing to compare it to. Close to the shore you could really see how fast the boat moved. We all stood along the railing, watching the shore go away. Then the Proctor said that it was time for breakfast. We all went below deck. The Proctor waited and then he walked right behind me. I don't know if he did it on purpose, or if he was just bringing up the rear. I was last in line.

He did the same thing at breakfast that he had done at dinner. It made more sense this time, because we were eating with everyone else on the boat. They were all waiting in line with us. When I brought my food back to the table I bumped into one of the other boys and I knocked his coffee over. Somebody made a joke. They asked me why I didn't get off the boat now, instead of last night. It was pretty funny. Everybody laughed.

The Proctor had told us to bring our books to the mess. We were going to have our first class after breakfast. I remembered him telling us, but somehow I forgot to bring them. I was the only one who forgot. I hadn't even noticed everyone else carrying them. I thought maybe I could go back after I was finished eating, and nobody would notice. But as soon as I stood up, the Proctor asked me where I was going. I told him that I was going to the bathroom. He said that I was going to get my books, wasn't I? I was surprised, because I hadn't realized that he noticed when I forgot my books. He didn't seem upset, though, so I nodded. He shook his head, and gave me a look. It's a look my Father gives me sometimes. It's a very disappointed look. It's funny. The Proctor had told me to bring my books, but he was acting like it said something that I forgot them. That I had really showed him who I was. That's what my Father would say, whenever he made that face. I had really showed him who I was. But it was always about things that I didn't care about, that weren't my idea in the first place. I don't know. It's just funny, I guess.

I went back and got my books. I couldn't find my notebook, and I lost some time rummaging around for it. Then, I found it. Then, when I went to leave, the Proctor came in. I thought maybe they had decided to have class in our quarters. But it was just the Proctor. I had my books, and so I held them up so that he would see that I had them, now. But he didn't make any sign that he noticed them. He said that he needed to talk to me. He had that very serious expression that people get when they want you to know they aren't mad anymore, because you're just an issue and they need to find a way to deal with you, and getting mad it beside the point. He wanted me to know that he needed my help. He couldn't do all the work alone. There were too many boys. He needed to know that everyone was doing what they should be doing, otherwise he couldn't give the other boys the attention they deserved. If he had to focus all of his attention on just one boy, then the others would be shortchanged. He said it very matter-of-factly, like we were talking about trading bunks. I said that I wasn't trying to cause any problems or take attention away from anyone else. I really didn't want to cause any trouble. Things just kept happening. He nodded, but you could tell that he was just agreeing because he didn't care what I was saying. He just wanted me to promise to be good and then shut up. It made me mad, because I *was* good. But I couldn't even tell him that. He just stood there, waiting for me to agree. So I agreed. I hated doing it, because it was like admitting that before he had asked me to be good I had been trying to give him problems. There's a legal word of it. It's called allocution. It was actually pretty clever of him. He made me allocute by promising not to do what I had been doing, like I had been doing it on purpose. For a minute I couldn't even be mad, because I was so impressed.

But right after that I got really mad. I was walking behind him down the hall, watching the back of his head. I could see the line above his collar where his last haircut had grown out. What I mean is that the hair on the back of his neck was starting to grow out. It wasn't the hair that made me angry. I don't really know how to describe it. I guess I was mad that someone with their last haircut growing out like that could talk to me the way the Proctor had. That's not quite it either, though. It was more like the rest of the Proctor was so official and so put together. Everything about him had the School behind it. Even his face was the School. The hair on the back of his neck was the only thing that wasn't. It was the only place where, if I'd complained, nobody could have said that I was wrong. Even the School would have been embarrassed by the hair on the back of the Proctor's neck. I walked behind him, staring at the hair above his collar and hating him.

I didn't notice it, but while I was walking I bunched the cover and the first three pages of my notebook up into a tight ball. The top and the bottom had ripped out of the spiral. When we got back to the mess hall I smoothed them back out. You could still tell what I'd done, though, from the ripped pages.

I didn't realize until I got back to the mess hall that I hadn't taken my pill with breakfast. I'm supposed to take them with every meal. I had meant to take it when I went in to get my books, but when the Proctor came in I forgot. I remembered that back at the hotel I had put one in my pocket, one that I had never ended up taking, but it was the pocket in one of my other pairs of pants, and they were back in our quarters. But I couldn't go back now so I just sat there, listening to the lesson. But I wasn't really listening, because I was too distracted by thinking about how I hadn't taken my pill. I was sure it didn't matter, because I was just going to take one at lunch anyway. But for some reason I couldn't stop thinking about it.

The other reason I wasn't really listening was because the motion of the boat was still making me feel a little bit sick. It was funny, because when I wasn't thinking about it it didn't bother me at all. But after I noticed it, I couldn't help feeling it. It was really frustrating, because after the way the Proctor talked to me I didn't want to make things any worse. But I couldn't help it. The Proctor called on me to answer, and I didn't even know what question he had asked.

Then, it happened. The Proctor called on me again, but I still hadn't been listening. I really wasn't feeling well. He called on me and when I didn't answer he gave me the same look he'd given me before, that disappointed look. Nobody said anything, because everyone was looking at the Proctor and me. Then, one of the boys said that I was quite an individual. That made a bunch of the other boys laugh. The Proctor glanced at them, but then he went right back to looking at me with that disappointed look. He really wanted me to feel terrible, I guess. I was feeling too sick to feel terrible, though.

Then, right as the Proctor was starting to say something, I threw up. I threw up right in the middle of the circle we were all sitting in. All the other boys jumped up out of their chairs. Even the Proctor jumped back. But I just sat there, still in my chair, throwing up. I was really sick. My body kept trying to throw up, even when I didn't have anything left in my stomach. Then, that stopped. Everybody was really quiet, because I had kept throwing up after they had all finished yelling and now it didn't make sense to make a lot of commotion.

Then the Proctor came over. After I finished throwing up I closed my eyes because I was feeling very tired. But the Proctor shook my shoulder, and so I opened my eyes. I followed him back down the hall to our quarters and I got into bed. I tried to explain that it wouldn't help, that it was the motion of the boat on the water that was making me sick. But when I opened my mouth, nothing came out. I was too tired to figure out how to say it. Then the Proctor left and I fell asleep.

I woke up when everyone came back after lunch. I had slept through lunch, but I wasn't feeling well enough to eat anyway. The Proctor brought me some motion sickness pills and a sandwich. It was really nice of him. I took one of the pills and ate some of the sandwich. I was feeling a little bit better. Then I took one of my regular pills. I was glad that I had remembered. When I was younger I got so nervous before School on some days that I would get sick. When I was sick, I didn't have to do anything. They let me stay in bed and watch movies. All they wanted was for me to get better, and all they wanted me to do was stay in bed and rest. Even though I was sick, I remember being happy. I felt a little like that when the Proctor brought me the sandwich.

After lunch everyone went back out again, and I stayed in bed. I wasn't tired, though. I felt a lot better. I got up and got dressed. Most of my clothes were School uniform clothes. I had to look for a while in my bag until I found some clothes that weren't. After I was dressed I left the quarters. I knew that everyone would be gone for a while, and that they wouldn't notice that I had left.

I didn't go back up toward the mess hall, or up on deck. I went the other way down the hall. I went down a ladder and ended up in the engine room. There was a long catwalk running between the engines. The noise that we hadn't recognized, but that one of the boys said was the engines, was a lot louder. I went down the cat-walk to another ladder, and then I went up. I came up outside the bridge. I didn't go in, though. There were a bunch of people standing around, and I knew that they would ask me what I was doing. I went down and through another door. Outside of that door was the outside. It didn't go out onto the regular deck, though. It went out onto the upper deck, up where the bridge was. From up there I could see a long way in every direction. There was nothing but ocean. It was cold outside. The wind was blowing hard, and that made it feel cold. I couldn't tell if the wind was blowing against us, or if it was just that we were moving so fast. Away from land you couldn't tell how fast you were moving. Seeing the ocean, I started feeling bad again. I didn't just feel like getting sick, though. It's hard to explain. I had this feeling that I sometimes have. When I have this feeling, the only thing I can do is close my eyes and think really hard about something calm, about something safe and familiar. I thought about the sound the ball made on the rackets, while the boys played tennis. Thinking about that, I felt a little bit better. But when I opened my eyes the ocean was still there, and I started feeling that way again. So I went back inside. Inside I felt a lot better. I was happy that we were on such a big boat, that I could spend the whole time inside and hardly ever have to go up on deck.

Right as I started going down the ladder to the engine room, somebody called out to me. It was one of the Sailors from the bridge. I guess he'd seen me when I walked past the door. I went down another rung but when he called out again I stopped. I didn't know what would happen to me, but it didn't seem to matter very much. So I came back up the ladder. It was kind of funny. Once I was standing in front of him, he didn't really seem to know what to do. I said that I had lost my group, and that I was trying to find my way back onto the deck, because I thought that was where they were. Then I got worried, because I realized he might want to take me where I said I was going, and then I would have to be back on deck. But the Sailor seemed relieved when I talked first. After that I knew I didn't need to worry, because he thought I was just a lost kid. He told me to go down another ladder at the other end of the hall, and that would take me right there. I started walking down the hall, and then halfway down I turned to make sure he'd gone back into the bridge. Then I went back and went down the ladder into the engine room.

It was hard to be quiet, walking on the catwalk. The catwalk made a lot of noise when you stepped on it. For some reason I started walking faster and faster. It doesn't make any sense, but it was like I was trying to get away from the noise. Then pretty soon I was running, and of course the noise was much worse. It echoed around inside the engine room. Then I stopped running, because I got to the ladder that led up to the hallway by our quarters. I went up fast, because I was worried that someone had heard me and was coming to yell at me and ask me what I thought I was doing. But nobody did.

I came up into the hallway. It was really strange to go from the noisy engine room to the quiet, empty hallway. I thought that maybe everyone had come back while I was away, that the Proctor was looking for me. But when I got back to our quarters it was still empty. I didn't want to be there alone, so I went down to the mess hall, looking for the rest of the boys. But the mess hall was empty, too. I went past the mess hall and out the door leading onto the deck. I thought it would be fine if I didn't look at the ocean, if I only looked at the deck and where I was walking. That didn't do any good, though. Even without looking at it, you could tell the ocean was everywhere. I tried to think about the sound the tennis balls made on the rackets, but it didn't really help. I couldn't close my eyes because I was walking and looking for the others, and without closing my eyes I kept seeing the ocean so that the sound of the tennis ball didn't make any difference.

The others weren't up on the deck, though. I didn't know where else they would be. I went to the railing and tried to look straight out, only looking at the sky and not looking at the ocean at all, but I couldn't do it. Then I tried looking just at the ocean. I looked right down from where I was standing. I tried to pick one wave, and watch it until it broke. I couldn't do that either, though. The waves all changed all the time. They didn't break, but just went flat and then came up again in a different place. You couldn't really say that it was even the same wave. It was all the ocean, though. Looking at the ocean like that, I didn't feel bad at all. All of a sudden, looking at the ocean felt a lot like sitting with my eyes closed, listening to my parents play tennis. No one was looking at me or telling me to do anything. I could just forget that I was even there. It was a big relief.

Then, I sort of slipped. I was kind of leaning over the railing, and I slipped. I wasn't really leaning over the railing, though. What I was doing was I had climbed over the railing and was leaning out from it, holding on with my hands behind me. After I stopped feeling bad when I looked at the ocean, all of a sudden I wanted to just look at the ocean. I didn't even want to see the boat where it touched the water. I wanted to see just the ocean, like the boat wasn't even there. But right away, when I hit the water, I didn't want to just look at the wa-ter anymore. I wanted to be home, I wanted my Mom and Dad and I didn't want to ever be away from them. I started screaming back at the boat. The boat was moving away pretty fast, though. Away from it, you could really tell how fast it was moving. Plus, they couldn't hear me over the sound of the engines. I started swimming after them, but it was pretty obvious right away that I wasn't going to catch them. I wouldn't have been able to get back up, even if I did. I didn't know where the ladder was. I kept screaming, though. I wasn't thinking very clearly.

But then, all of a sudden, the engines stopped. The boat kept moving for a little bit, but then it slowed down and it didn't really seem to be getting much farther away. Then I heard another engine start. It wasn't really an engine noise, though. What I mean is the noise wasn't big enough to be an engine. It was just a motor noise. Then, a little while later, one of the lifeboats from the deck came over to me. I was pretty tired, but when I saw it coming I felt better. The Sailor in the lifeboat pulled up next to me and then pulled me into the boat with him. I lay at the bottom of the boat, feeling cold. The Sailor gave me a blanket, but pretty soon that was wet and so it just made me colder.

Everyone was up on the deck. They pulled the boat up and the Sailor and I got out. The Captain shook the Sailor's hand. The Proctor did, too. All of the other boys were looking at me. I was feeling really cold by then. Then the Proctor came over. He took me down the hall to our quarters and told me to get some dry clothes and take a shower. I did and when I came out everyone was gone, at dinner. The Proctor was still there, though. He told me that he had already spoken with my Parents, and that arrangements were being made for me to go home. He said that the boat was going into port the next morning, and that I was going to get off and stay at a hotel. I was supposed to talk to my Parents about getting a plane ticket home. I thought he was going to say something else, but he didn't. He looked at me with the same disappointed look he had given me before, the one my Father always gives me. Then he told me to go eat dinner. I went down to the mess hall and ate dinner. Some of the Sailors had already finished, and I sat at their empty table. I sat with my back to everyone, facing the wall.

The Proctor took me to the hotel. He waited until I checked in, then he left. I went up to my room and sat on the balcony. The hotel was close to the ocean, but I was on the other side. My balcony looked out onto the courtyard. There were men working in the courtyard, trimming the hedges and digging in among the flowers. I thought about the other flowers, at the other hotel. I wondered how they were doing, if the frost had come again. Eventually the frost comes to everything, and there is no more worrying or wondering what will happen. I wondered what would happen to the boat after it was gone. I was glad I was off and that now I was in a room that didn't face the ocean. I went to the bathroom and took my pill. It was almost dinner time. I'm supposed to take them with every meal.

Weakness

I wake up at four forty-five so that I can get to the gym by five, when it opens. I love having the weight room to myself. Most other guys, even the ones who lift early before they go to work, don't come in until six. For one hour everything is clean and the gym is almost cold from the air conditioning and everything is where it should be. My usual routine is light cardio and then weights: upper body on Mondays and Wednesdays, lower body on Tuesdays and Thursdays, core on Fridays. I don't have a set routine for the weekends, I just try to make sure I break a sweat. This weekend Krista wants to go on a long bike ride, so this weekend it's that. Other weekends I play basketball or go for a run. I try to do something different every weekend. If you do any one thing for too long, eventually your body adapts and stops responding to it, and the exercise becomes less effective. Then you get weaker without even knowing it.

I leave Krista sleeping and go out without turning on any lights. At the gym I sign in at the front desk and go upstairs. There's only one other guy in the gym, and he's running on one of the treadmills. They're playing a top forty radio station over the speakers, but you can't even hear it over the sound of the treadmill motor and the guy's steps. It doesn't matter, though, because in a minute I'm going to be doing the same thing. I get on the treadmill a few down from him and start my circuit. I usually do fifteen minutes, just a little more than two miles. I start at seven miles-per-hour and then push it up another half-mile-per-hour every minute, until I'm going at twelve miles-per-hour. Then I work my way back down until the fifteen minutes is up. Sometimes, when I get bored, I play with the incline. I'll go a half-mile at a slight grade, then another half at a higher grade, then sprint at no grade, and then finish by climbing at a moderate grade. Today I just do my usual circuit, though. There is a row of mirrors in front of the cardio machines, and a row of TVs above that. I start off watching my form in the mirror, making sure I'm using my upper body to power my lower body. Then, when the pace starts getting higher, I watch the TV so that I'm distracted and not thinking about how bad it is and how much it sucks. This never really works, but it sort of works.

This morning I can see the other guy in the mirrors, and when the pace gets bad I start to watch him instead of the TVs. He looks like he's probably my dad's age. He's still running at the same, fast-jog pace he was at when I came in. He's wearing those really short running shorts with the high slit and I can see all the bandy muscles moving under the skin on his thighs. He's got his mouth hanging open with that blank, long-distance run look on his face and as I push the pace up another half-mile-per-hour I start to hate him and his stupid face and his stupid running shorts and the dumb little hiss sound his water bottle makes when he squeezes water into his mouth. Then I max out at twelve and I don't think about anything except getting through that minute, and how I don't have to hold out forever, just until it's over. Then that minute is over and I start to work back down. Then I'm finished and I walk around the room with my hands on my hips, hearing my pulse in my ears and trying to get control of my breath, with my legs all rubbery and loose beneath me.

I like to take a few minutes to let the lactic acid break down, and to give my body a chance to metabolize some sugars, but I check the time and it's already twenty after five. I hate going right from cardio to weights, because you're always weaker right after. Sometimes waiting five minutes is the difference between putting up a hard set and thinking you've lost strength. I don't have time to wait, though, because I told my mom that I would be at the house at six fifteen. So I go right to weights. The weights are on the other side of a partition, and once I move around it I try to forget about the other guy, even though I can still hear him. For a second I wonder how far he's running, and then I think how stupid it is to do long-distance running on a treadmill. The big benefit of a treadmill is that you can get a short cardio burst and then move to other forms of exercise, all in the same space. Thinking that, I start to get annoyed by the motor sound and the sound of him running. I start thinking that I made the extra effort to come in early so I could have the place to myself. I want to go over and say something to him. But then all of a sudden the motor winds down and stops, and the gym gets quiet. I wonder if the guy is going to come in and lift, but then I hear the door close and I know I'm alone and it's the best feeling in the world.

I do the first series of crunches and then move on to weighted side-bends. Then I do a light set of good mornings, then a heavy set, then more weighted side-bends and another set of light good mornings. It's important to work your back when you work your abs. People think that a core workout is just about your stomach, but they're wrong. If you only work your stomach you start to get imbalances. This can lead to all sorts of problems. I always work my lower back and obliques as much as I work my stomach. I finish with more crunches and some hanging knee-raises. There's still no one else in the weight room, so I lift my shirt and check my stomach in the mirror. I'm only twenty-five, so it's a lot easier for me to get definition. After a while it gets almost impossible to keep it. I've seen enough older guys who do pretty much what I do that I can guess what I'll look like in another five or ten or fifteen years. That's just the way it goes.

I go down to the locker room to take a shower and the guy from the treadmill is there, too. He's wet from the showers and he undoes the towel around his waist and starts to dry off. He dries his head and when he moves the towel all the hair on the sides of his head and the little wisps that are left on top stand up at crazy angles. The muscles in his arms move in that strange way that they start to when you get older and your skin gets loose, where the muscle moves one way while the skin moves the other way, always chasing and never catching what's underneath. I get undressed and get into the showers and I can feel my stomach tightening from the workout and I'm glad that I'm young. For a few minutes I forget everything and just stand under the water, glad that I'm young. There's nothing better and when it's gone there's nothing else.

I want to stay in the shower, but I have to get out. It's already almost six, and so I get dressed without getting all the way dry and I don't stop to talk to the girl at the front desk when I leave. It's cold outside and I can feel the cold get down inside my collar and up under my hat and everywhere I'm not all the way dry. The sky is pale behind the trees, but the sun won't be up for another half-hour. I get on the highway and push it little bit, because the road is empty going the way I'm going and because I'm running a little bit late. But then up ahead I see flashing lights and so I slow down. I wonder for a second if someone coming in off the third shift fell asleep at the wheel, but then I get close I can see the cop by the driver's window.

I get off at the next exit and there's no one at the intersection so I roll through the stop, turning right. My parents live about a mile from the highway, but back in a development. What I mean is that it doesn't feel like it's right off the highway. I park on the street and walk up the driveway and go in without knocking. I can hear my mom moving things around in the kitchen and for a second I stand in the hall not making any noise, because I'm not ready for them to know that I'm there. But then my mom turns around and sees me and jumps, and we laugh and for a second it feels like I just dropped in to see her, like it's one of those nice surprises.

"Oh, Guy," says my mother. "I didn't hear you come in." She checks her watch and says, "You're so punctual."

"Hi mom," I say. "How's dad?"

"He's all right," she says. "He's asleep."

I say, "How are you?"

"I'm all right," she says. "I'm as well as I can be, I guess." She wraps her arms around her middle and shivers, even though it's not cold. "I appreciate you coming with us," she says. "So does your father."

"Of course," I say. I can feel my torso tightening up from the workout as I talk, and I feel better because it reminds me that I'm strong and that I can handle anything. I ask my mother if my father is ready to leave.

"Almost," she says. "We just have to wake him up and get his shoes on."

I follow her into the living room. My father is asleep in his chair, and I go over and stand next to him and say, "Hi, dad," but he doesn't wake up.

"I'm just going to run to the bathroom," says my mother. "I won't be a minute."

"Dad," I say when she's gone, this time loud enough to wake him. He opens his eyes and looks around and then at me and I say, "It's time to go. Let's get your shoes on." I kneel down at his feet and I start to undo the laces on the shoes my mother has set out. While I'm doing that I hear the bathroom door open and hear my mother coming down the hall.

"Did you get his shoes on?" she calls.

"I'm doing it now," I say.

She comes into the room and kneels next to me and says, "Bill. It's time to go now. We need to get your shoes on."

My father just looks at us. When he looks at me I look away and when I look back his eyes haven't moved. Then my mother lifts one of his feet and his attention shifts to her and what she's doing.

"I've got to put your shoes on," she says. "It's time to go. Our appointment is in less than an hour."

"Oh. Kay," says my father.

"Guy," says my mother, "help me here."

I lift my father's leg at the calf, and I'm surprised again that now my fingers almost touch on the other side. My mother starts to hurry.

"Wait," she says, "let me get it all undone first. You don't have to hold his foot up the whole time."

"It's fine, mom," I say. "It's light."

"But it's probably not very comfortable," she says.

"It's fine," I say again.

"For your father," she says, not looking at either of us, looking at the shoe in her hands.

"He's fine," I say. "Let's just go."

We get both shoes on and then we help him stand. He's unsteady across the carpet and pauses before the stairs. I climb the first stair and lift, holding him under the arm, as he steps up beside me. My mother is behind him, steadying him. Then we reach the top and my mother goes out to get the car. We wait inside and I feel the close warmness of my father's armpit on my hand. Then the car appears out of the garage and we leave the house and begin the long shuffling walk down to the driveway, down to where my mother is waiting.

"All right," says my mother, taking the buckle as I hand it across his chest, after we've worked him in. "Off we go."

"Oh. Kay," says my father.

I close his door and get in behind him. Through the bars of the raised headrest I can see the pink and white scar running down the back of his neck. I stare at it for a long time, a lot longer than I want to, because there's no time for aversion, or thinking about what you would like to have happen, and because it's only by forcing yourself to do what you don't want to do that you get stronger. But then we drop down from the driveway to the street and his head sways like an infant's, and I'm sorry that I have been watching. I stare down at my hands.

"You know what," I say. "Can you stop? I think I'll follow you down. I told grandma I'd take her for groceries this afternoon. I may have to leave early. Is that all right?" But it isn't a question, because I am already opening the door and getting out. "I'll follow you," I say. "Just go ahead. Don't worry. I know how to get there. I'll be right behind you." And then I close the door and I can't keep myself from jogging to my car.

I let them leave the development before I start after them because for a few minutes I feel lightheaded. It's because I didn't eat anything after my workout. I usually bring a bar or a shake, or I pick one up at the gym minibar, but because I was running late I forgot. When I start after them they're already gone, and I figure they're already on the highway. I realize that I don't know the way, not really, and so I start after them and hope that I'll catch them or remember the way once I see it.

It takes me forty-five minutes to get downtown, and I don't see them. Traffic is really heavy, though, so I figure that they're just somewhere up ahead of me, and that I can't get to them because of the other cars. I see the hospital from the highway, though, and I get off at the right exit. After that I get lost driving around the campus, and so I park and I ask the woman at the desk in the first building I come to for directions. She tells me that there are a few oncology wings, that they are divided up by the kind of cancer. She asks what kind of cancer my father has and I hear myself say that he has stage four melanoma with distal metastasis. She nods and tells me where to go. I go to the next building and ride the elevator up and when I get off I see my father sitting in a wheelchair by the desk.

"Hi, dad," I say.

"Hi," he says, and he sounds even more tired than he did at the house.

"Where's mom?" I say.

"Par. King," he says, closing his eyes between syllables.

"Where do we need to go?" I ask, taking the chair by the handles.

"Mom," he says, "knows."

When my mother gets back I ask how it was getting dad into the wheelchair and she tells me it was no problem, that someone helped her. After a while they call our name and we go behind the door and down to one of the rooms. Then we wait some more. Then, after a long time, a nurse comes in and starts to set everything up. She checks my father's arms for veins and then she swabs the insides of his elbows.

"I'm going to insert this needle into your arm," she says, holding it up to show him. "Then I'm going to start the flow with saline, before we start the Dacarbazine. Once that starts we have to just let it go. It'll take about an hour for it to run all the way. Does that sound all right?"

"Yes," says my father.

"Is the doctor going to see us before you start?" asks my mother.

"I can go see if he is available," says the nurse, "but I know he usually comes in while the treatment is already in progress."

"I know that," says my mother. "I was wondering if he was going to come talk to us before you started the Dacarbazine. I talked to his assistant, and he said that the doctor was concerned about running the Dacarbazine because of the way it might interact with the other drugs he's on."

"I don't know anything about that," says the nurse. "No one said anything about it to me." She is fingering the inside of my father's left arm, and he is watching her. "I'll tell you what, though," the nurse says. "I'm going to get him started on the saline, and then I'll go see if I can find the doctor. He has to run on the saline for a few minutes anyway. That way we can talk to the doctor before we do anything."

"Ok," says my mother. "Thank you."

"Thank. You," says my father. The nurse pushes the needle into my father's arm and I watch his face and his expression doesn't change at all.

"Ok," says the nurse, taping the needle down. "We're all set here. I'll go see if I can find the doctor."

After she leaves my mother goes over to my father, holds his hand and kisses the top of his head. He follows her with his eyes and when she kisses him his eyes close. I remember again that I haven't eaten anything since my workout, and I think how important it is to eat right after, because if you don't it takes a lot longer to recover.

"I'm going to go down to the cafeteria," I say. "Do you guys want anything?"

"Can't you stay until the doctor comes?" says my mother. "I want you here. You always remember things that I forget."

My father says something, but his voice is too low and too raspy for me to understand. I ask him to repeat what he said and he says, "Stay."

"You know the doctor isn't going to come for forever," I say. "It always takes them a million years to get here. I'll be back before he shows up."

"Can't you just stay?" says my mother. "Just stay because I'm asking you to."

"I haven't eaten since I worked out," I say. "I need to eat something."

"I think I have something in my purse."

"I'll just be five minutes," I say. "Even if the doctor comes while I'm gone, I'll be back before he leaves."

Neither of them say anything, and so I go out and down the hall. I think I remember where the cafeteria is, but I get lost and I wander around the halls until I find a sign that points me in the right direction. Finally, I find it. It's still early, and the lines aren't that long. I get my tray and I ask the man at the grill if he can just grill me two chicken breasts. He says he doesn't have that. I ask him if he has anything besides hamburger patties and he says he has turkey burgers, so I order two of those. I'm going to tell him to leave them off the bun, but I go and get a water from the cooler and when I get back the two burgers are already made. I go up and pay and then I throw the buns into the trash and eat the two patties together. Then I finish the water and head back to the room. When I get there the doctor is coming out and my parents look at me. They don't say anything. They just look at me.

"What did the doctor say?" I say. There is a rhythmic hissing as the machine pumps drugs into my father's arm. "What did he say about the Dacarbazine?"

"He said it was fine," says my mother. She's not looking at me anymore. She rests her head on my father's shoulder and closes her eyes. I sit down in the chair in the opposite corner. The patties feel heavy and sour in my stomach and I wish that I had bought two waters instead of one.

"How does it feel?" says my mother. "Does it hurt?"

"No," says my father.

I stay for thirty minutes, and then I have to leave. I have to leave because I told my grandmother that I would take her for groceries at eleven, and it's already ten. I leave a little bit early so that I don't have to rush on the drive. As I'm pulling up in front of their building a song I like comes on the radio, and I have time to sit and listen to it. It's a song I used to listen to whenever I was trying to get fired up for sports or anything. After the song ends I go inside and my grandmother is asleep on the couch. I go over and wake her and she looks at me apologetically. Her shoes are on the floor next to her feet. Through the open bedroom door I can see my grandfather, still in bed asleep.

"It's the darnedest thing," she says. "I sat down to put my shoes on because I knew you were coming, and then I fell right asleep."

"That's all right," I say.

She sits up and starts to pull her socks on.

"All of my socks are so tight anymore," she says.

"Are your feet swollen?" I say, because her feet have been swollen lately.

"I don't think they're very much worse," she says. She is working her right foot into the shoe, rising from her seat to push her foot down and in. I tell her I am going to be right back and I go into the bathroom to wash my hands and face. When I come out she has both shoes on and is working to tie them. I find her grocery list on the table and I put it in my pocket.

"Do you need a jacket?" I ask.

"Is it cold out?"

"It's not too bad," I say. "You can see what I'm wearing."

"Maybe I'd better," she says. She is working her way to the edge of the couch, pushing herself up from the cushions. Then she stands, and I watch her sway before she finds her balance and walks to the door. "How was your father today?" she asks.

"He was all right," I hear myself say.

"Where did I leave that jacket?" she says.

We go out to the car. I hold her door and then wait as she maneuvers her way into the seat. There are other residents out on the grounds and I watch them until I hear her say that she is ready and I close the door.

"Everyone is jealous that I have you to take me to the store," she says when I get in. "Everyone else has to use the shuttle. And that only goes to the store in town."

"I know," I say, because she has told me this before. She reaches over and pats my hand on the steering wheel.

"I do so appreciate you taking me," she says.

"I'm happy to do it," I say.

"So your father was all right today," she says.

"He was all right," I say. "He's certainly not getting any better."

"Oh," she says, "I wish they'd find something that would work. You hear about things all the time, about this thing or that, that just does the trick. It's so maddening. You just don't even know what's out there that you're not trying." She has her purse up on her lap, and she is going through it while she talks. "Oh no," she says finally. "Honey, we have to go back. I up and left my grocery list."

"I've got it," I say.

"You do?" she says.

"Yeah," I say. "I grabbed it off the table. That was your list, wasn't it?"

"On the dining room table?"

"Yes. On the yellow pad?"

"Oh. I suppose that was it." She pats my hand again. "Lucky we have you along," she says.

We pass the main residential building, then climb the hill and come out onto the main road. I wonder if my parents have left the hospital yet. I think that they probably have. I think about calling my mother to ask how the rest of it went. I don't see how he's ever going to get better, being poisoned like this, and I wonder if the doctors are only treating him because we expect them to and because we will pay and because there's nothing else to do. Then I start thinking about how doctors never say what they mean, and about how there's no way to make them say it. So I think fuck the doctors. If he's going to die then there's no reason to poison him. There's no reason for him to suffer, just because they can't say what they mean. But then I think, You don't know anything, and there's nothing you can do about it anyway.

"You know what I have to get that I forgot to put on the list," says my grandmother, "is cornmeal. Your mother gave me her cornmeal muffin recipe and I was going to make some last night but I didn't have any cornmeal. I thought I did but then I went and looked and wouldn't you know it, no cornmeal!" She laughs, and I laugh with her.

"I'll write it down when we get there," I say. "Remind me."

"Then we're really in trouble," she says, and we laugh again.

"I'll remember," I say.

We park, and I wait as she collects her things and gets out. She waves at the checkout girls as we go in and they wave back at us. I take her list out of my pocket and hand it to her. She looks it over and decides where we need to go. I follow behind her, pushing the cart. When she struggles to lift a melon from the bin I help her, and I am surprised by how light it is. Her fingers sag under the weight of each new thing she places in the cart.

"I don't know what I'd do without you," she says again. "It does get tiresome, the way grandpa is anymore. I do need a little break now and then."

"How was he today?" I ask, even though we all know how he is.

"Oh, Guy," she says. "Well a lot of the time he's like you just saw him. He's sleeping half the time. But when he's awake he's just so angry. I don't know what to do. You hate to see him like that. He's positively transported. And about the silliest things. You know, things he can't do a thing about. But wouldn't you know, that's the thing that's got to be fixed and by golly, he's the only one who knows just how it should be done. He was so upset this morning because he went into the bathroom and noticed that cord, you know, that they have so if someone falls or some such thing they can call for help up to the main office. You know, he saw that and it was all you heard about. It's not something new, you know! He was so upset about it! He just. Oh Guy, I just don't know what to do about him. I hate to leave him alone at all. You just don't know what he's going to do anymore." She starts to lift down a gallon of milk, and I take the handle and do it for her.

"It's nice to have a strong young man helping you, isn't it?" says a woman waiting behind us.

"Oh, it's just wonderful," says my grandmother. She pats my arm and smiles up at me. "I'm lucky to have him. He takes me every week. Otherwise we'd go hungry."

We all laugh at this. I push the cart out of the way so the woman can get to the milk. My grandmother is looking at her list. I look over her shoulder, trying to figure out our path through the store. The woman behind us smiles at me as she goes past. I pick out a dozen eggs and check them for cracks.

"I do so appreciate you taking me," my grandmother says, again.

"It's no trouble," I say.

"You didn't have any classes today?" she says.

"No," I say. "I've got a test on Friday, so they gave us this week off to study. And I don't work until tomorrow night."

"That's nice," she says. "Nice that they give you time off to help your grandmother."

"What does he want them to do about the cord?" I say.

"Oh, I don't know," she says. "He's just ranting and raving. There's nothing to do. I try to tell him that, but does he listen? You bet he doesn't. No sir. He's going to call the management and set them straight by golly. He's going to get things done."

"We need to find something for him to do," I say.

"Don't I know it," she says. "But he won't do anything. I try and get him up out of that chair. It was a beautiful day yesterday. I tried to get him to go for a walk down to the end of the road. Would he do it? Not on your life."

"Huh," I say.

"And it wouldn't be so bad," she says, "except that he's convinced that he still can do so many things, and you just can't, at our age. When we were up to Syracuse that last time he was convinced that he had to do something or other up on the roof. I thought he was going to break his neck. Can you imagine? Crawling around up there on the roof? I pretty near went crazy worrying about him. But would he listen to me? Uh-uh."

It takes us an hour to get everything. When we get back to their apartment I tell her to go in, that I'll carry everything. She tells me she can carry some things and I pick up all the bags to show her that I can and that it's no trouble. So instead she goes in ahead of me and holds the door.

Inside the apartment my grandfather is up and watching the news. I take the groceries out of the bags and set them on the counter, and then I ask my grandfather if he wants to play checkers because it's something we do sometimes and because I can't help my grandmother, because I don't know where anything goes. He doesn't hear me ask, though, and so my grandmother yells to him to turn down the TV, and when he does she tells him that I want to know if he wants to play checkers. I get the board out and start setting it up and while I'm doing that he comes over and sits down.

"How are you feeling?" I ask him.

"Oh, fine," he says. "Is it your move?"

"It's my move," I say, and move one of my pieces.

He looks at the board for a while and then says, "Is it my move?"

"I think so," I say. "I just moved here, so I think it's your move." I point to the jump he can make. I watch his face until I see him notice it. He reaches out to take his piece and jump me, but his fingers are trembling too badly. After a couple of tries I take the piece and move it for him. "You got me," I say. "I don't know where I was on that one."

He laughs, then moves again.

"You seem like you're doing better," I say. "Grandma says you're eating."

"I can't put any weight on," he says. "I'm still all bones." He holds up his arm to show me the loose skin hanging down in a flap like a fin running from his wrist to his elbow. "None of the doctors can tell me why."

"You're not doing anything," I say. "Even someone young will lose muscle mass if they don't have anything to do with themselves. Have you been out to the garden? Grandma says they're planting now."

"That's no garden," he says. "Have you been up to our house in Syracuse?"

"Not for a while," I say. "But when I was a kid, I was up there every summer."

"Sure," he says. "Then you remember the garden your mother had I mean your grandmother had up there. That was a garden. This garden they've got here: a bunch of people planting stuff right on top of each other and no sort of order or anything. What they ought to do they ought to have it so everyone has their own garden spot. They could do it, too, for what we're paying to live here. Do you know what we're paying?"

"No," I say, "I'm sure it's plenty."

"Plenty is right," he says. "And your grandmother has to go out there with a hundred other people. It's ridiculous. Fifteen thousand dollars we pay a month to live here, and your mother can't even have her own garden."

"Terrible," I say.

"Terrible is right."

"Whose move is it?" I say. "I think it's my move."

"I wanted to talk to you," he says. "You know that we're paying fifteen hundred dollars a month to live here, and what do they have in the bathroom but a pull chord if somebody needs help. Can you imagine, fifteen hundred dollars a month? For that much they ought to have someone who comes in and checks on you. And they could do it, too. They could have a nightlight in every room so that at night a nurse could come in and check on you to make sure you're all right. Not this shit they've got here." All of a sudden he's started crying, and I wait while he gets his handkerchief out of his pocket and blows his nose. "Not this shit they've got here," he says again, when he's got himself back under control. "Your grandmother could fall in the shower and couldn't reach the cord and then what? What the hell are they gonna do about it? Nothing. They're not gonna do a damn thing. And you can bet – I'll bet you a million dollars to a nickel that they're not gonna do a damn thing about it. I can afford it. I'll bet you that much that they're not gonna do anything."

"I think they want to make sure they respect your privacy," I say.

"What they ought to do," he says, "is tear this whole place down and build a Cleveland Clinic. Down in Florida they got three Cleveland Clinics right within fifty miles of us. That's what I think they ought to do. They could build a Cleveland Clinic and anyone who was sick, they could go there and it wouldn't cost them anything. They could see a doctor and get whatever medicine and the medicine would be delivered right to their house for free. They could do it, too. And the government would pay for it. This country is the greatest country in the world. People nowadays talk about this is the worst recession. Let them try to live through a depression! That was *hard*. Times were *hard*, then. My father – we used to have milk delivered and it was nine cents a quart. I want to tell you this. It was eleven cents a quart and then – it was nine cents a quart and when they raised the price to eleven cents my father quit and he went up the road to a farm that was up there and he could get the milk for five cents a *gallon*. Wasn't pasteurized or nothing. I can remember that. Your mother thinks I'm nuts. I'm not nuts."

He starts crying again, and I wait while he searches through his pockets, trying to find the handkerchief in his lap. I can hear my grandmother coughing in the other room. I ask him if he'd like a ginger ale and when he nods I go into the pantry to get it. Once I'm inside, though, I lean back against the wall and close my eyes. I can hear my grandmother coughing and my grandfather blowing his nose. I wonder what the nursing home I end up in will look like. I wonder if it will be like this one, and if when I'm living there I'll lose my mind and start rambling about nurses and nightlights and hospitals that don't exist. I wonder if my skin will hang in loose flaps from my bones, if I'll spend my days watching news programs that I can no longer understand. I know that I will, know that all of these things will happen because time is stronger than you and you can't push back against it. Then I take the ginger ale and go back out.

"Don't you have any ice?" he says, when I set the can down in front of him.

"Sure," I say. "I'll get you a glass."

"And get one for your grandmother, too."

"I don't think she wants one."

"All right. Are you having one?"

"I wasn't going to," I say. "I try to stay away from refined sugar."

"You're too skinny," he says. "What are you worried about that for?"

"I don't know," I say from the kitchen, though I know he probably can't hear me. I fill a glass with ice and bring it and set it next to the can. "I think it's your move."

He looks at the board for a while, then moves. I move and he jumps me again. In the other room my grandmother is still coughing.

I stay for a couple of hours, drinking coffee and listening to my grandfather. Then I tell them that I have some things to do, and I leave and go home. I don't really have anything to do until Krista gets off work at five. I think about going for a run, just to kill time. I don't feel much like running, though, so instead I do a yoga dvd workout that Krista's mom gave her. I don't usually do yoga, but it's good to know different kinds of workouts. When I put the dvd in it comes on in the middle, where Krista stopped it last, and the instructor is talking about one of the poses. There's a man and a woman standing behind her, doing the pose the instructor is describing, and I watch them and try to do what they're doing. I follow them through a series of poses and then follow them while they repeat. While we're repeating the instructor starts talking about letting go of tension and anxiety, about breathing in time with the movements. She says to think about anchoring my fingertips and toes into the ground, to push against the earth as though I could move it. She says to think of my body as a series of links in a chain, all bunched and bundled together, and that as I move through the poses I should visualize the chain becoming long and straight, and all of the links lining up. She tells me to feel my breath restoring me to health and tranquility.

After that I still have a little more than an hour before I have to get ready, so I sit down and look over my notes for Friday's test. The test is on musculature and function. For the first part we have to name and identify the muscles of torso, and list which muscles they directly interact with. The next part is an essay about how we would create a workout program for an individual based on his or her needs and stated goals. It's all pretty straightforward. After that there is a series of true and false questions. The true and false part is the easiest part. When I was a lot younger I always had trouble with tests. Then, when I got older, I realized it was all a matter of discipline. When I was younger I never studied for anything. When I got older I made myself study. Now, I don't even think twice about it.

Discipline is like any other kind of strength. The more you use it, the stronger it gets. Then, when you really need it, when you have to do something that you really don't want to do but that you know has to be done, you can make yourself do it without a problem. Then all the time you spend training it is worth it, because you're strong when you need to be.

I study for forty-five minutes, and then I go in to take a shower and get ready. The water in my shower takes a while to get warm, and while I'm waiting I stand in front of the mirror and check myself over. My arms look about the same but my triceps don't seem as pronounced and I make a note to change back one of the exercises I had changed in my routine. Then I look at my torso from a bunch of different angles. The mirror is on the medicine cabinet, so if I open two of the sides part of the way and leave the middle closed I can see almost all the way around. I look at my arms again, and decide that maybe my triceps don't look less pronounced. I can't really tell. The lighting in that bathroom is funny. I decide to do both exercises next time. I think about how my father's arm looked, when the nurse pulled up his sleeve to insert the needle. I check the water and it's warm enough, so I get in. I'm still thinking about my father's arm and then I start thinking about my grandfather's arm, and the loose skin hanging down now where the muscle used to be. He worked in a shop his whole life, and then he retired and his body stopped being any good for work. That wasn't so bad, though. For a while it was just that his body couldn't do what he asked it to do anymore. But now it's something else, too. The weakness isn't just in his body anymore. I run my hands over my torso and feel all the muscles tensing under the skin.

I get out of the shower, dry off and get dressed. I've still got some time until Krista gets off work, but I've got nothing else to do so I decide to go down early anyway. It's just starting to get dark. I wonder where we are going to go and I think that probably Krista will insist that we all go to Taste. She won't have to insist too hard, though, because all of the girls she works with like it there. There's a new girl coming out, too, so I'm sure that they'll want to show it to her.

I see her from across the floor and I stay out of sight until I'm right behind her. She gives a little squeal when she sees me and she puts her arms around my neck and kisses me, and while she does that she picks her feet up and I hold her like that. She still has fifteen minutes left, though, so I tell her I'm going to go look in the health and nutrition store next door and come back. She blows me a kiss as I leave and all of the girls she works with are watching me, and it's the best thing I've felt all day.

The guy working at the nutrition store is somebody I know from the gym where I used to work out, before Krista and I moved into our place and I started working out at the place where I work out now. He's a lot bigger than he used to be and I tell him he looks good even though I'm thinking he's probably on steroids. He's wearing a sleeveless shirt and I can see acne on his upper arms, near his shoulders. That's one way to tell. I tell him he looks good anyway. We talk for a minute about lifting and he tells me all about how much he's putting up. I tell him that I've been studying musculature and physiology, and that I'm not interested in lifting heavy anymore. I tell him I'm more interested in functionality. I can tell he doesn't care, though, so after a few minutes I tell him to take it easy and I leave and I go wander around the mall for ten minutes, until Krista calls me and tells me she's done.

"How was it today?" she asks, when we're out in the car and alone and together.

"About the same," I say. "How was work?"

"Shitty," she says. "I got two thousand in, but Jan stole probably another thousand from me. I went to the bathroom and when I came back she was ringing out some people that I had been helping for half a fucking hour." She's checking her makeup in the mirror.

"You should tell somebody," I say. "She keeps doing this."

"They don't care," she says. "It's not going to make any difference. Plus she's the - whatever they call her - the floor manager, so she's just going to tell them that she was helping them as much as I was, or that I flaked when it came time to ring them out. It's total bullshit."

"So what can you do?" I say. "There has to be something. It's ridiculous that this keeps happening."

"There's nothing you can do," she says. "I just keep hoping that maybe one day she'll get hit by a car on her way into work. I'm serious. I'm not even like that, but I wish that she would just die."

"Ha," I say.

"Anyway," she says. "I don't want to talk about it, because I'm out of there, and tonight is going to be fucking amazing, and Jan can fuck *off*."

"What do you want to eat?" I say.

"I don't care," she says. "I'm not that hungry."

We go to a sushi place that's nearby. It's where we went on our first date, and when I say so Krista says I'm sweet for remembering. It takes half an hour to get a table so we sit at the bar and Krista has a vodka and Red Bull and I have a Jack and Diet Coke because they don't have sugar-free Red Bull. When we finally get a table Krista says she still isn't hungry, and so I order a couple of sushi rolls that I know she likes and a couple that I like, so that she can have some if she wants. She's texting with the girls from work and so I just sit there and wait for her. When our food comes Krista says she has to go to the bathroom and so I start without her and I eat all of the sushi that I ordered for me before she gets back. When she gets back she calls me a pig and I say at least I didn't eat yours. Then she says that the girls are meeting up in fifteen minutes and that we should head over that way. I say ok and then I say that she should eat something if she's going to be drinking all night. She rolls her eyes and she eats a couple pieces. While she's doing that the waiter comes back and I ask for the check and pay so that when she's done eating we can go. The club is on the other side of town, and it'll probably take twenty minutes to get there, with traffic.

Krista gets a call right as we get into the car, and talks almost the entire way across town. I don't really care all that much, because I don't really feel like talking anyway. I'm angry with myself for not going running, because I don't feel like I got a very good workout from the yoga dvd. I think about the guy at the nutrition store, the one I knew from the other gym, and the way his shirt pinched in under his armpits because his shoulders were too big for the holes. Sometimes people tell me that I look big, but they don't even know what big looks like. I think about all the people who are so much stronger than me, and how much more I could be doing, and for a minute it's like I've been lying to myself and I just realized it.

We get to the club and I let Krista out because I can see all of her friends standing around outside. There are no spots anywhere, and I have to park two blocks away. It's cold on the walk, and my skin feels tight and I feel better and I know that I haven't been lying to myself. When I get to the club they're all still standing around, waiting for me, all shivering in their skirts. Krista introduces me to the new girl, whose name is Gina. I know the other girls already. We have to yell at each other because the club is so loud, even outside. Gina says she's worried because she has her sister's ID. She's only twenty. We go up to the door and the bouncer, the guy checking IDs, is a guy I know from another gym where I used to work out. We haven't seen each other in forever, but we used to push each other a lot when we lifted together. He lets us all in without checking anyone's ID and I can feel how relieved and impressed Gina is and everybody else, too, because everyone wanted Gina to come and he only didn't check because of me. One of the other girls, a girl named Meg, says she's buying everybody shots, and so we all go to the bar and it takes about ten minutes to get served. While we're waiting for our drinks Brian, the boyfriend of another of the girls, a girl named Haley, shows up. I know Brian a little bit. We all do our shot and then Gina says she wants to buy everybody's next drink. Haley says she wants to dance before she has another drink and the other girls all say they want to, too. Brian and I stay at the bar while the girls go dance, but we can't really talk because of the noise. I don't know what to say to him anyway. He works for his dad's company, selling some manufacturing component. We don't have anything in common.

After a while I get bored waiting around for the girls, so I yell to Brian that I'm going to go try and find them. He says he'll come with me. It takes us about ten minutes to move from one side of the room to the other, it's so crowded. Plus Brian keeps falling behind in the crowd, and I have to wait up for him. When we finally find them they're all dancing together except for Gina. I ask Krista where Gina is and Krista gives me a look and points and I see Gina off in the crowd being grinded on by this guy that we don't know. I look around at the other girls and they all look concerned but then they shrug and so I don't worry about it. One of them goes to tell Gina that we're all going to go get another drink and I see her nod and then tell the guy and I see the guy shake his head and for a second he holds her elbow and won't let her go. But when she pulls away he smiles like he was only kidding and when she comes over he comes with her.

We head back to the bar and the guy following Gina buys us all a shot. I don't think I'm watching him but then Krista grabs me by the hand and yells for me to forget him and come dance with her. We all go out on the floor and dance for a while. I keep an eye on Gina and Krista acts annoyed and then she acts hurt that I'm paying more attention to them than I am to her, and so I stop watching them. Then I see Gina push the guy away and he stumbles back into some people and one of them spills their drink on him. He gets up in Gina's face and I can hear him yelling at her even over the music and so I grab him and shove him away. He starts yelling at me and he pushes me back, and then I shove him again and he falls down, but he's hanging onto my shirt. We go down and he ends up on top of me and hits me once before I get back up and then I swing for his face and hit him in the side of the neck. Then one of his friends or somebody grabs me from behind and so I throw my head down and try to flip him over my back. But he hangs on and I go down again, and then the guy who was yelling at Gina starts kicking me and the guy holding me is still holding on and I can't pull away. Then finally I get loose, and I tackle the other guy and then there are bouncers right on top of us and I'm being pulled out of the room and someone is yelling in my ear for me to cool it, just cool it.

Then I'm outside and I'm trying to tell one of the bouncers, not the one I know, what happened, but he tells me to be quiet because he's on the phone with the police. Down the block two of the other bouncers, the one I know and one I don't, are talking to the other two I was fighting with. I can see a big red mark on the side of the one's neck, where I hit him, and the other one is bleeding from the nose and I think I probably did that when I tried to throw him over. The one who yelled at Gina keeps adjusting his shirt because the collar is all stretched out, and I check my shirt and find a big tear under my right arm. It's a shirt Krista gave me for my birthday, and I yell at the two guys that the one owes me a new fucking shirt. I'm going to say more, but the bouncer puts a hand up and shakes his head at me and so I sit back down. I sit there for a while, wondering what's going to happen and wondering where the girls are. Then, a little while later, a police car pull up and the cops get out and leave the lights on.

Across the street, people have stopped to watch. Other people yell things at us as they drive by. I keep trying to tell the bouncers and the policemen what happened, but they keep telling me to sit down, to back off and shut up. I don't, though, and after a while the bouncer I know comes over and puts an arm around my shoulders and tells me he knows what happened, that these guys have been a problem before, that I just need to calm down and shut the fuck up and he'll take care of it. I thank him about fifty times and then I sit down to wait. After a while I guess they let Krista out and I show her the rip in the shirt she gave me.

"That's ok," she says. "Are you all right?"

"I'm fine," I say. "How's Gina?"

"Gina's fine," she says. She looks down at the two guys, and the one blows her a kiss and I stand up to yell but then I remember what the bouncer said and I sit back down. "Assholes," says Krista. "What a pair of fucking assholes."

"Yeah," I say. My hand is starting to hurt, and I wonder if I landed on it when I fell or if I hurt it when I punched the guy in the neck. I want to have hit him in the face, for him to still be unconscious, and the fact that he's not pisses me off more than anything. Krista is texting someone, the girls inside probably, and she starts rubbing my back with the other hand.

Then I see the policemen and the bouncers shake hands, and the policemen go back to their car. I stand up as the bouncer comes over and he says, "It's all right, but you should probably go."

"Sure," I say. "Sure. Thanks. Thanks a lot. Really. Thank you."

"All right," he says, nodding. Over his shoulder I can see the two other guys walking off in the other direction. One turns and sees me watching them, and yells something I don't hear because the bouncer is saying, "All right man. Let's get going."

Krista and I walk back to the car together, and it takes a long time because Krista is wearing heels and she can't walk very fast in them. I keep thinking that we're going to run into the two guys, and for a while I hope that we do so that I can fuck them up the way I wanted to in the club. Then I start to hope that we don't just because Krista is with me, and I worry about what might happen to her. So I try to hurry her up, but she gets mad at me and says she's going as fast as she can.

Finally we get to the car. There's no traffic on the highway, but it still takes a long time to get back to our apartment. Krista is texting with the girls, and she tells me that Gina says thank you for standing up for her.

"It's all right," I say. "I mean, it's no big deal." The adrenaline has worn off and all of a sudden I feel sore and exhausted, and I just want to be in bed and asleep. I want to not have to think anymore, about anything. I want Krista to rub my back again, and for her to tell me that I won the fight and that even if I didn't that it's only because there were two of them.

But I also want to go to the gym and put up the heaviest set imaginable, to pump my arms and legs and back and chest until all of my muscles feel useless and full of sand. I want to run until I throw up, to go until there's no energy left in my cells for thoughts or feelings or anything but drawing breath and pumping blood. Then I want to take the last hour, the last month, the last year, take all of the things that happened since my dad collapsed at work and my grandparents moved up here and pile them together like stones, into a huge mound. Then I want to throw these things as hard as I can, harder than anybody else ever could, against the flow of time so that they get lodged somewhere and never happen, not again, not ever.

But I know I can't do that, and that it's stupid to even think it. We get home and get into bed, and Krista kisses me goodnight and then falls asleep. I stay awake for a while, just thinking, and then I fall asleep too, not knowing how anything will turn out but knowing at least that I am young, that I am strong, that I can handle most things.

Set Up

They meet in the usual way: someone, by chance, knows both of them, and is meddlesome or self-assured enough to act as fate's go-between. This is how he thinks of all matchmakers: as in their own minds witness and assistant to something grand and sacred. He agrees because he is alone, because he has not been with anyone in months, because when faced with such circumstances, he tells himself, one may only agree. The matchmaker in this case is his sister, unwaveringly kind to him and invested wholly in his happiness, and he does not wish to disappoint her. The girl in question is someone with whom his sister works, and is seven years younger than him. Speaking to her on the telephone he makes a joke that he is sure she will miss or misconstrue, but to his surprise she laughs. They make plans to have dinner and then attend a party to which she has been invited.

Dinner is brief and uneventful. She talks, almost exclusively. When she is not talking he asks her questions. He learns that her parents are still living and still together and reside near his own parents. He learns that her maternal grandmother is ill. He learns where she attended college and what she studied there. He is grateful to her for carrying the conversation when he can think of nothing to add, though he is certain that to her he must seem dull and ineloquent, must seem the very sort of person who would be alone at his age.

The party is being thrown by a friend of hers from work, and his sister is also in attendance. She gives a lively and welcoming shriek when they arrive. She hurries off with their coats and returns with a glass in each hand. She encourages them into the room with the comic manner of a mother shooing her children from the kitchen.

The lightness of this moment, the sense that they are the focus of a benevolent attention, leaves in its passing a pervasive uncertain anxiety. What should he do? The room is crowded and everyone is shouting to be heard over the music playing on the stereo. He tries to think of something to say, of somewhere to go, but finds that every path is blocked by bodies and furniture, and everywhere they would go is already occupied. In the car they fell with what was to him surprising ease into a familiar and unmannered conversation: she spoke with no apparent awkwardness or hesitation and he, finding her at ease, felt something like ease himself. This fragile comfortable air hung about them as they climbed the stairs and did not dissipate until his sister shrieked, thrust glasses into their hands and ushered them, comically, into the room.

Suddenly, standing amongst the partygoers, silently lamenting the evaporation of whatever intangible connection had begun to form and still feeling acutely the effort of the dinner conversation, he is exhausted by the prospect of this evening. The hours that stand before him seem tiresome and convoluted, strained and uncertain, and he longs for the moment when, whatever awkward goodbye they enact completed, he is free of the self-consciousness her presence demands and is allowed to sink, mercifully, into the dreamy and selfless nothingness of his own thoughts.

He recognizes this desire as the very soul of what has become his sister's consistent criticism in recent years: that he is "too inside his own head." She has made it her mission to "draw him out," to help him engage with people, but if there is a sense of necessity in this it is all her own: he is happy in his own company, and finds that he receives little nourishment from interaction; little enough, at least, to make prohibitive the cost such activities demand in time and effort. He has rarely, for example, had a conversation that intrigued and inspired him like the work of Hugo or Balzac, has rarely met anyone who hours later lingered in his thoughts like Heathcliff or William Wilson. He has rarely, in fact, if ever found life to be as rewarding as its fictional mirror, rarely been moved by his own experiences with a force rivaling that achieved by the works of Thoreau or Whitman and this fact now, long-known but drawn suddenly again to the fore, convinces him anew that the evening's plans are a mistake, that he would do better to feign illness and allow the girl her passing disappointment than force her to endure an evening of his deteriorating interest and mood.

Yet of course he does and says nothing: he continues to consider the room, hoping to discern what it is that he should say or do.

The girl speaks, but he cannot hear her over the music and voices, and he asks her to repeat herself. She does not hear him, and replies with a confused expression. She points to a hallway leading off the main room and then starts towards it. She is met at every step by a coworker's shouted salutation and he has the sense, by observing these, that she is the sort of girl toward whom all of her coworkers feel a fraternal duty and affection. They consider him quantitatively, cooly, and again he feels exhausted by the prospect of the evening and wishes to return home.

Finally, their haven is reached: the narrow space at the end of the hall, beside the bedroom in which the coats have been piled, offers some escape. Far from the stereo speakers they are able to converse in something like their normal voices. By now it has occurred to him what a stupid venue a party is for a first meeting, and he is annoyed that they came. They should have gone elsewhere, somewhere where they would not have to shout to be heard! He says as much, and is surprised by her objection: she has been looking forward to this party for weeks, and wouldn't have missed it for the world. He suddenly sees himself as he must seem in this moment to her: so pompous as to assume a meeting with himself more important, more desirable than a gathering of her friends. He retreats awkwardly, over-assertively, insisting that it is only the noise and his wish to talk more freely to her, with no need to hide in the hall or shout over the others, that prompted the observation.

Knowing her only briefly, he is unsure whether she is satisfied by this explanation. He sips from his glass and, finding it empty, offers to fill hers as well. When he returns she seems to have forgiven his unintentional gaff. She wipes with a napkin a spot that has appeared, at some point on his walk from the kitchen to the bedroom, on his shirtfront. Afterwards they stand in silence, allowing the music from the other room, which in this corner of the house comes to them as no more than a vibration, to excuse their reticence. He again tries to think of something to say or do. He feels ridiculous and drinks nervously, hardly paying attention as he does so. She warns him, in an almost matronly way, that he has to drive her home later. He sets the glass down on the counter in the adjacent bathroom in nearly comic acquiescence.

She asks him if he would like to dance. They move back to the living room and into the middle of the floor, where a space has been cleared and in which a few other couples are dancing. He thinks, as they begin to move together, of other girls with whom he has danced, and of the ridiculous things he thought as he did so. He is happy to be free from youth's frantic assertion that life and its experiences are more meaningful or important than they are. There was one girl, the first girl, for whom he felt everything, and with whom the moment of dancing had seemed the culmination and completion of his young existence. When she did not reply to his professed love as he hoped she would reply something had changed in him, so that each subsequent girl had inspired in him something less than the overwhelming and imbuing and nearly hallucinatory dream of Love and what it meant to be Young and in Love. Which was ridiculous, of course, for naturally it was not love he had felt for that girl but some teenager's sentimental misunderstanding, and so it was no real thing that was diminished when she did not reply as he hoped she would.

Still, he finds this phenomenon endlessly poignant: finds innumerable compelling insights into himself and his subsequent life when he considers this early heartbreak. The problems in his marriage, with all its talk of Alienation of Affection, seems somehow directly birthed from this early experience. It is clear to him now that his then newly-formed and still-malleable understanding of women and romance were greatly impacted, and that now the archetypes in his mind still retain that girl's mark. Is he capable of love? He has wondered previously, but now does so with acute accusation.

While he considers all of this the stereo continues playing, and they keep dancing. She places her head on his shoulder in a gesture which, knowing her only briefly, he does not dare interpret. He considers it as though from outside himself, from outside the small circle their steps make on the carpet. Others are watching them. What are they thinking? He recalls their fraternal manner, their cool reception. How should he reply to the girl's gesture?

His discomfort, the feeling that he is trapped in a situation in which he cannot artfully maneuver, turns quickly into frustration and from frustration into anger. Why does his sister insist on meddling in his affairs? Of what interest is it to her that he go on dates or meet people? His reclusive tendencies, his reticent demeanor have, at the very least, never turned (as he has observed that they sometimes do) into a depressive state, have never come to demand of his relations time or effort or worry. What right have they then to attempt to influence or alter him? He subsists in his own world and is, if not happy, then at least comfortable. It is none of her concern, after all, how he occupies his hours!

Her insistence that he behave more like her, the constant and subtle assumption behind her actions that he must see the world as she sees it, must react to things as she reacts (and must be, therefore, nearly completely miserable in his situation), suddenly annoys him with a ferocity he finds surprising. After all: he has known for some time that his sister (with her conversational ease, her social calendar, her various clubs and committees) does not and cannot understand him, does not and cannot understand the bliss and release that solitude affords him. It has been many years, however, since he has felt that his sister's myopic view, when resting upon him, somehow obscured its object: many years since he felt somehow negated by her misunderstanding. He has the sudden urge to do something utterly, incomprehensibly rude or odd, something for which the other partygoers will seek out his sister for explanation and for which she will have none.

But of course he does nothing: a new song begins, and they continue dancing. Her head continues to rest lightly on his shoulder, and he continues to allow it to. He has, on second thought, no desire to disturb the party or the partygoers, nor any wish to ruin the beautiful (if incomprehensible) gesture the girl has made. He closes his eyes, attempting to forestall any thoughts of the future and their attendant anxiety. He is, for a moment, simply a man dancing with a girl, and for that moment he is flooded by a vague and nearly effervescent sense of himself and her and all that this scene might blossom into and become. It is with effort (and, he cannot deny it, sorrow) that he reminds himself that, after all, life is not a movie: that very little dramatic ever occurs, and more often than not whatever true drama life holds is wholly overshadowed by its participants' insistence that something important and meaningful has happened. To infer from her gesture (her head upon his shoulder) she has fallen in love with him would be the acme of foolishness, of naivety and immaturity. To infer that she wishes to sleep with him is, perhaps, only slightly less absurd. To assume that anything means anything at all...

He cannot finish the thought. He does not know what it means, nor can he imagine any future in which this ignorance does not cause some regrettable misstep. Dropping her off at her door he will lean to kiss her and she will retreat, embarrassed by the misunderstanding that has occurred between them. He will not attempt to kiss her, and instead learn later (from his sister, he thinks, and cannot suppress an involuntary frown) that the girl wished very much to be kissed (of course his sister will not say as much, but she will not have to: he will know by the very fact that the girl has mentioned anything that he acted incorrectly). Or, perhaps, when kissing her he will suggest that he come inside, and she will here recoil, insulted by the suggestion that she might be so easily had. Or he will not, and realize later (after further consideration) that he should have. Every action seems incorrect, founded finally on nothing save his own faulty and unreliable reading of her manner.

He doesn't trust himself to know, nor does he have the constitution to act regardless. He is filled with envy of the other partygoers, all who seem seamless and untroubled by any anxiety regarding the prospect of incorrect action. Often enough he has looked spitefully down on the same attributes he now covets. How he wishes that he could act without regard for self, with no sense of shame, as an animal acts! A beast is never asked why, never called to task for the decisions it has made. He feels the hanging weight of his own trial, at all moments being held and in which, at any moment, the prosecutor, in the guise of anyone, may demand of him the reasons for his actions with the unquestioned and unquestionable backing of society as a whole.

Someone laughs nearby and he looks around, certain they are laughing at something he has, without noticing, done. But of course they are laughing at something that was said by someone else about something in no way, it seems from their behavior, related to him. Returning his attention to the matter at hand he finds that he has lost and cannot reclaim his previous train of thought.

The song ends. The girl excuses herself. She weaves her way away through the crowd, presumably to the bathroom. He moves out of the open patch of floor where they have been dancing. He goes to the kitchen to get another drink. In her absence he feels for the first time that those watching him are impressed: that his being here with her makes him a character of some distinction. He puts ice in his glass and searches through the bottles. He has the sense that at any moment one of the men standing nearby will make some vaguely affirmative comment, will ask how long she and he have been dating, will ask some misinformed but suggestive question. It is exciting and pleasant to think that in this moment the eyes of the room are turned with benevolent envy upon him, and he has only to hear the slightest hint to know beyond any doubt that such is the case.

Someone taps him on the shoulder, but when he turns it is only his sister: she has made her way through the crowd to catch him in the girl's absence, to ask how it is going. His annoyance and disappointment (that she is not one of the men nearby, expressing with graceless questions his admiration and envy) are quickly replaced again by fatigue, this time at the prospect of explaining himself. He replies, summarily, that it is going fine. His sister is delighted to hear it. She is so glad that he decided to come to the party. She knows that he hates it when she meddles. She only does it because she wants him to be happy. He replies that, at the very least, he knows that.

He moves out of the narrow kitchen and back into the room, ostensibly to be away from the crowd and to hear his sister more clearly. In truth he has moved because his happiness is quickly being replaced by embarrassment: he does not want the others in the kitchen, who have perhaps been viewing him with benevolent envy, to hear what his sister is saying.

Yet it occurs to him in the short distance between the kitchen and the room's far wall that perhaps everyone already knows everything, that his sister after all works with these people, and keeps nothing to herself, and once again he is filled with frantic embarrassment. He sees himself, suddenly and acutely, as the ridiculous figure he must seem: self-possessed and reticent, he is nevertheless divested of any and all interiority; himself explained, in the vocabulary of the eternal extrovert, as something he had no wish to be. He imagines his sister explaining to everyone that her brother is coming to the party, that he is a bit peculiar and "too much in his own head," if they know what she means, but is really a sweet guy and nobody to think twice about...

The girl returns from the bathroom, yawning and apologizing, saying that she was up very early that morning and if it is all right with him thinks that she had better call it a night. He goes to get their coats and returns to find her talking with one of the men from the kitchen. There is an awkward moment before they are introduced. The man has worked with the girl for several years, and makes no comment to suggest his benevolent envy. The girl takes her coat, putting it on before he can offer to help. He wonders if he has done something wrong, but then thinks better of it: very likely her changed manner has nothing to do with him. They leave and he holds the door as she gets into the car.

She is quiet on the ride home, and he wonders again if he has done or said something to upset her. Soon he is certain of it. He wracks his brain, attempting to divine what it might be. Perhaps she misheard something, and took offense? He thinks of what he said, and how it might have been misconstrued. After several blocks he has still thought of nothing.

Then it is too late: they have arrived at her building. She does not move, and for a moment he thinks that she is waiting for him to say or do something, before he realizes that she is asleep. He touches her lightly on the arm and she opens her eyes, and at once begins rapidly explaining and apologizing. She really was up very early that morning, and did not sleep well all night! She was rather nervous about their date! Oh, what a stupid thing to say! It's just that she doesn't go on many dates. And now she has ruined their date by falling asleep, simply because she was too nervous to get to sleep the night before!

Her admission fills him with impervious confidence, and he assures her that the date is far from ruined. If she feels like she needs a second chance, should they try again next Friday? There is a movie playing that he has heard is very good, and there is a restaurant he knows near the theater. She quickly and nervously agrees. She opens the door and begins to get out but then, in a gesture that surprises him, leans back inside and kisses him swiftly on the lips. He discovers that he has involuntarily closed his eyes, and opens them again when he is startled by the sound of the car door closing. She waves to him from the doorway, then hurries inside. He remains at the curb, watching the building and hoping to see her light come on. After several minutes it is clear that her apartment does not overlook the street, and he heads for home. This minor disappointment does not diminish his mood in the least.

Back home, he wonders if he should have offered to walk her up. Wasn't that what people did? Was that what she was expecting? He reassures himself that she was tired, and did not wish for him to come up. His certitude on this point is uncharacteristic, and he allows it to wash over the memory of the entire evening, so that he feels for a brief and wonderful moment that he acted all evening exactly as he should have. This peace is quickly shattered by doubt: the girl's head on his shoulder, he realizes with startling disappointment, was a symptom of her fatigue and nothing more. He reassures himself that surely she must have felt something for him to allow this familiar contact, whatever its motivation. This explanation, however, does little to elevate his dampened mood. So instead he thinks of the unexpected kiss. He gets into bed, attempting vehemently to suppress the notion that the kiss was delivered out of apology, or duty, or any one of a number of diminishing interpretations.

Later that week he has dinner with his parents. They eat at a small restaurant which they have frequented as a family since he and his sister were young. His mother jokes with the waitstaff and the people at the nearby tables. His father watches her and says little. At the end of the night he argues cordially with his father over who should pay the check. Finally he succeeds in wrestling the slip from the older man's hands. His father protests but, he knows, is and always has been infinitely pleased by these gestures. On the drive home one of the tires goes suddenly flat, and his father directs him as he puts on the spare. Back at their house his father goes into the other room to make arrangements for the car and he sits at the kitchen table while his mother makes the coffee. She asks him, casually, if he is seeing anyone these days, and he knows instantly that his sister has told her everything, that there is no detail to which his sister is privy that his mother does not now know.

Neither his sister nor their parents ever cared much for his wife, and he has thought for a long time now that it was precisely those characteristics which they found unfamiliar or objectionable that so intensely attracted him to her. She was nothing like them, and as such seemed to him capable of providing a stimulation which their life never had and, he believed then, never could. The greatest irony was, perhaps, that when their marriage ended he had no real sense for why it had: that that which was mysterious in her had remained mysterious. This was, at that particular moment, a realization of sickening defeat, for it solidified in his own mind his place as one of *them*: his years of private, smirking righteousness as he saw himself standing beside his wife, imagined that they shared a secret and profound and unnamable connection, while all around stood his family and their friends, neighbors, coworkers, all wearing expressions of stupid confusion, evaporated into a joke when he saw that he, too, after all, had never understood her and, it seemed, lacked the capacity as much as his mother or father or sister. Her request for the divorce seemed to be her assertion that he was *not like her:* that he had failed, finally, to become a person like her and unlike his family, a person he wished vehemently to be. He was well into his thirties before he realized fully the fallacy inherent in the attempt itself, but by then the sting of losing her had faded, and it was an easy realization to make.

The realization that he was irreducibly himself, that it was absurd to attempt to alter his unconscious proclivities, had sounded in his mind like a great barred door sliding closed. His self, then, was a prison cell from which there was no escape. Later, after living with the knowledge that the self was a prison from which he could not escape for several years, he again considered this realization and found that it sounded in his mind like a great wooden door swinging closed and latching. The self, no less a prison, had now become in his mind a comfortable enclosure with a stout wooden door. More years passed and, considering the realization once again, he found that it sounded like a gate being closed: a gate over which he could easily see and, on some occasions, and for varying intervals, jump.

The third and final image, the most pleasant in the series, wavered and fell away only in moments of profound opposition or scrutiny: when he was called to account for himself for something he had said or done, or when he was considered with great attention by his mother, sister, or father. At these moments the very core of his being seemed to be on trial: when he was called to task he would wish reflexively to be someone else, someone who would never have done or said the thing that he did or said; when his mother looked at him it was with an expression that dismissed all artifice, that bespoke a knowledge of him more profound than his own, that would not be fooled by any clever attempt to distract or mislead. He stood exposed, viewed once again through the prison cell's barred door, his back against a bare, immobile, whitewashed wall.

It is with this sudden sense of imprisonment that he listens to his mother as she repeats her question. She moves casually to collect the cream and sugar and arrange them on a tray. He thinks of the first girl with whom he danced, of how strongly he felt that he loved her then, of his momentary assurance that her presence was life's affirmation and reply to all of his inarticulate yearning. His mind seizes suddenly upon the notion that love is merely another form of self-creation: that people fall in love not with the other but with the idea of themselves as they seem when they are with the other. The profundity of this thought momentarily overwhelms all other stimuli, and for a moment he is no longer in the kitchen, no longer waiting for the coffee, no longer watching his mother set the tray on the table before him but off in his own thoughts, marvelously free.

The coffee is ready, and his mother sets his cup before him. She sits in the chair opposite and watches him. In the other room, his father asks the man on the telephone how much cheaper the tires are by the set. His mother repeats her question and he replies, in a playful and knowing tone, that he is certain she already knows all about it. She smiles and blushes, caught in her ruse. He laughs to show her that it's all right. In the other room his father asks if he can buy one tire now at the set price, and the three others at another time.

"I just want you to be happy," says his mother.

"I know," he says. "I am."

The Young Folks

When we got back to the hotel someone, one of the girls, said that she needed coffee if we were going to keep going like this. We went for coffee but Julia stayed behind. She'd had an ulcer the year before, and didn't drink coffee. Susan and Brett and I and a few of the others went without her and when we got back we found her smoking outside the lobby. It was pretty cold, and she was huddled back into a corner where the wind couldn't get to her. The others went inside and Susan and Brett and I stayed, and Julia offered her cigarettes around. She offered them to Brett first. After that Susan wouldn't look at Julia. Susan and Brett had dated for several weeks during the previous semester. Brett didn't take one and neither did I and Susan pretended she hadn't heard. After that Julia asked if we wanted a drink and we all said sure. Julia crushed out her cigarette and took Brett's arm and they inside. We followed and when they were out of earshot Susan asked me didn't I think Julia was an intolerable bitch.

"No," I said, "not an intolerable one."

She laughed and we caught them up. In the elevator Susan put her head on my shoulder. We went up to Julia's room and Brett made drinks and handed them around. He knew where Julia kept everything. Julia sat on the bed. Brett started telling a story that Susan had heard, and she laughed for him to stop. Julia said that she was intrigued, that she always loved Brett's stories, and so Brett continued. We all finished our drinks and Brett made another round. Julia called for them to be stronger, that she hadn't even felt the first one. Brett told her he would make her feel it, and Julia giggled. Brett came back with the drinks on a tray in a tableau of a waiter. Everyone appreciated the joke. I took one and so did Susan and Brett did too and Julia said, a toast to the happy couple, and we all raised our glasses and drank. Susan made a small squealing noise.

"Too much gin," she said.

"Drink up," Brett said.

Susan did as we told her. We all drank, too. In the silence you could hear the ocean against the beach out-side. Then Julia put on some music, and you couldn't hear the ocean anymore. It was music that we all liked. We sat and listened. I finished my drink and went to make another. Brett was leaning against the wall by the bottles. He nodded at Julia and grinned. He asked me to fix Julia another drink. I went back and got her glass from the bedside table. The song ended, and then an-other started. It was a song I didn't like, but everyone else seemed to like it very much, so I didn't change it. I fixed the drinks and brought them back. Susan was swaying with the music. I sat down beside her on the couch. Julia took her drink and raised her glass at me. Brett moved from his spot on the wall and sat beside Julia on the bed. Susan looked up at me and then glared at Julia. She did it for me to see. Julia didn't notice. She and Brett were talking. I asked Susan how things were going.

"Marvelous," she said, "it's never been better." She didn't say it sarcastically.

"You're drunk," said Julia. I coughed into my sleeve. Julia took another cigarette and Brett lit it. Susan slouched beside me and the ice in her glass spun and clinked together. I took the glass from her. Julia laughed for no good reason. Susan snorted. I went and filled Susan's glass at the sink and brought it to her. Julia leaned back against Brett and they stared at the ceiling together.

"I got a letter from John," said Brett. "I wonder if I have it on me." He felt his pockets. "I must have left it up in the room. Anyway, he sends his love."

"I love John," Julia said. She was speaking to the ceiling. "But then, I've always loved a man in uniform. We should write to him. Right now. All of us together. Let him know that we're thinking about him. Show him all the fun he's missing."

"I imagine it's a challenge for him to get mail," I said.

"He doesn't get mail," Julia said. "Only sand."

Brett snorted. Susan sat up and began to look better.

"Drink some water," I told her.

"No," she said. "I'm all right. I wasn't so bad before. I'm just tired is all. I think I'd like another drink. Just a little one."

I took her glass and went to make it. Brett was looking at Julia's neck. I made Susan a drink. No one spoke for a while. Then Julia put on another song. It was a song we all knew. Susan started crying. We all looked at her. Brett stood up but Julia put a hand on his arm and he sat back down.

"She's fine," Julia said. I put my hand on Susan's back. Then the song ended. Julia stood and turned the music off. Susan said that she was sorry.

"It's the gin," she said.

"Come on," I said, "Let's go down and get some coffee. The walk will be good for us."

Julia said that it was a good idea. Brett sat on the bed. I helped Susan up and Julia walked us to the door. I looked back at Brett and he winked at me. Julia invited us back afterwards but I said I thought I would just turn in. Susan wiped her eyes with a tissue that Julia handed her. We left. Susan was very unsteady on the way to the elevator. She didn't seem drunk, only unsteady. Riding down she asked if I wouldn't mind walking with her along the beach. I said I didn't mind and we went back down to the lobby and out into the courtyard. The beach was just beyond, across the road.

"I just don't know what's wrong with me lately," she said. "It's so silly. I was so proud of myself that I didn't cry during the ceremony. And now this. Oh, well."

We walked for a while. It was cold out on the beach, and I thought probably Susan would get cold before I did, and want to go back. But she didn't seem to notice. She seemed to be thinking about other things.

"She's terrible," Susan said all of a sudden. "She lets people believe that she cares about them. She's going to do it to Brett, you just watch."

"She cares," I said. "She just doesn't know what to do about it." I had known Julia for a long time.

"You're right," Susan said. "I shouldn't say such awful things. I'm her friend, after all. You shouldn't say awful things about your friends. But she knows how it is for me with her and Brett. Still, I shouldn't."

"It doesn't matter," I said.

She was quiet for a while. The beach was empty and the moon was out and shining on the water. We walked a long way, until I couldn't see the hotel. We walked down to where the beach ended against some rocks and Susan started climbing and I followed her. There were empty bottles and seaweed strands and dried-out crab bodies in among the rocks. I put my hand into one of the dark places between and came back with a half-dozen silver-gray .22 shells. I figured that somebody must have been firing into the ocean and I put them back. Higher up I found some more. They were scattered around on a flat gravel patch. Susan had already cleared the rocks and was making her way between the dark houses. I caught up with her as she reached the street on the other side. She started walking back towards the hotel. She had her collar up and her arms crossed tight over her chest. The wind blowing in off the water was cold and her hair and the scarf she had tied around it were blowing out almost straight and the ends were flipping over and over each other.

I fell in step behind her. She stayed pretty close to me for most of the way. Then as we got closer she began to move out ahead. I thought she might rather be alone, so I slowed down and let her get pretty far ahead. When she reached the lobby doors she turned around and looked back but I called to her that I was going to sit outside and have a cigarette and that I would catch up with her. She went inside and I watched her through the glass until I couldn't see her anymore.

After Susan was gone I couldn't remember where I'd put the cigarette I'd taken from Julia. Anyway, I didn't have a match. So I decided to go up to my room. But when I went inside Julia saw me. She and Brett had caught Susan on their way into the bar. They were waiting for me and so I went in with them. Once I was with them I didn't really mind.

There were some other people we knew in the bar. Paul was with Rita and Grant was there with a girl I had never met. Brett bought everyone a drink, and we never got introduced. By the time the drinks arrived he and Julia were being funny and everybody was watching them. Brett made a big show of doing a magic trick for the waiter. He put a napkin over his fist and waved his other hand over it. I could see some of the other people in the bar were staring at us, but no one else in our group seemed to notice or mind. We were sitting in booth with high walls and I could only see the other people in the bar because I was sitting on the end. Everybody else in the bar was much older than us, and looked pretty annoyed that we were there.

"Oh my goodness," said Julia. "Oh my. Oh Brett stop it. Oh I can't breathe." Brett was pulling a balled-up napkin out of his mouth. Everybody was laughing but Julia was laughing the most. She was making a bigger show of laughing at it than he was of doing it.

"Honestly," said Grant to Julia, "It isn't *that* funny." Brett came to the end of the napkin and dropped it back on the table.

"Oh Grant," said Julia, "don't be a prick."

I sat with them for another half-hour. By then the other people in the bar were starting to leave and with the drinks Brett was buying I was feeling pretty tired. I said goodnight and left the bar alone. When I was half-way to the elevators Susan caught up with me. We rode up together without speaking. Susan leaned against the back wall, and I could hear her dress rustling whenever she moved. The elevator was old, and I could feel the cables in the vibrations inside the car. I could feel the cable rhythm changing as we got closer to the top. I started thinking about all of the empty space in the shaft beneath us. Then the doors opened and she took my hand and led me out and down the hall to her room. She had left all of the lights on, and there were piles of clothes and hotel towels on the bed. She pushed the clothes off into the space between the bed and the wall.

"Sit down," she said.

I sat down on the edge of the bed. Susan went into the bathroom and came back holding the two water glasses with their paper caps. She set them on the desk and went to get the booze. She had left it out on the balcony to chill. Her hair was up and when she turned back to the desk carrying the bottles I could see goose bumps on the back of her neck. She filled both of the glasses halfway and then crouched carefully, pulling her dress to cover her knees, picking the mixers out of the refrigerator. She was making a big show of watching what she was doing. When they were ready she handed me my drink and sat down on the bed next to me. The mattress was soft and we fell in slightly towards each other.

"What are we doing?" I said.

"I don't know," she said. Her face was close to mine and then we didn't say anything for a while. Then we had to stop, because our drinks were in the way. Susan took them and set them on the bedside table and when she came back we went back to what we were doing. Then we fell back on the bed and she lay beside me and we stared up at the ceiling for a while.

"It's weird, isn't it?" she said.

"Yes," I said. I knew what she was talking about.

"I guess it's what people do," she said. "I guess it's what everybody does."

"Everybody we know," I said. "There's really nothing else to do."

"That's true. At least, I can't think of anything. Can you?"

"Not really," I said. "The whole thing feels so set, it's hard to feel one way or the other about it. I suppose I do want to, though."

"Me too," she said. "I always wanted kids, at least."

"I guess I want kids, too," I said. "But Jesus Christ, not for a while."

"What are you going to do before then?"

"I don't know," I said. "I wanted to be a writer for a while, but I couldn't think of anything that hadn't already been said better by someone else. Maybe I'll try to do that, though. I wrote one story that was pretty good. I showed it to my high school English teacher when I was home, and he said it was pretty good. So maybe I could do that."

"I don't know what I'm going to do," she said. "I'm not good at anything."

"I'm sure you're good at something."

"Nope," she said. "Well, I'm good at this. I'm good at being in school. I'm good at making professors like me. I'm good at making friends and going to parties. I'm good at being pleasant and sociable."

"Then you're one up on me."

"But what can you do with that?" she said. "What do I do in the real world, with talents like that?"

"Charm someone until they marry you," I said.

"And we're right back to it," she said. She propped herself up on one elbow and took a drink from one of the two glasses on the nightstand beside her. "What was it about?" she said. "Your story. The one your English teacher read. What was it about?"

"It was stupid," I said. "I thought it was good at the time."

"Tell me," she said. "You've got me all curious."

"You'll think it's stupid."

"Tell me."

"It was about this boy," I said. "It was just about this one day in his life. He's about nine or ten, I guess. He gets home from school and because he's bored he starts to look through his parents' things. At first he just looks through their drawers, but then he really starts to dig through everything. His parents are at work, and he ends up totally emptying out this one closet of theirs. The point isn't really that he does it, it's that as he does it he invents all of these other meanings for everything he finds. Anyway he loses track of time and his parents find him in their closet, with everything out on the floor around him, and they start yelling at him. Each time they see something on the floor, they say, "Oh no, not my whatever it was." That way the kid hears what everything is, and none of it is as interesting as the stuff he came up with. He's left feeling like his parents are these incredibly dull, ordinary people."

"I remember when I figured that out," she said. "What happens then?"

"Nothing," I said. "That's the end of it. The last scene is the kid imagining that someday he'll have a closet just like his parents' closet, and that his own son will look through it and imagine an exciting grown-up world, and the kid decides he won't tell his son the truth."

"It sounds good," she said. "Did you try to send it out? To magazines or anything?"

"I was going to, but I wanted to edit it first," I said. "I never got around to it. Maybe I will when we get back. I don't know. Honestly, I'm not sure it's worth it."

"One of my dad's friends used to write for the New Yorker," she said. "I bet you could send it to him and he would read it. He probably still knows some people over there."

"It's not good enough for the New Yorker," I said. "Besides, there are a million people writing these days. It's not like it used to be. Even if you're good, you're redundant."

"So you're not even going to try?" she said.

"No, you're right," I said. "Sorry. That would be great, if your dad's friend would read it. Even if he didn't send it to anyone at the New Yorker, at least then I'd know what someone like that thinks of it."

"All right then," she said. "You give me a copy when we get back, and I'll send it to him. It'll be better coming from me."

"Thanks," I said. "Really, thanks."

"Don't mention it," she said. "Like I said, socializing is one of the few things I'm good at." She yawned. "Oh God," she said. "Will you think I'm awful if I kick you out now? I'm about to fall over, and I've still got to figure my way out of this dress." She stood up and took the two glasses into the bathroom. I got up off the bed and went to the door. She came out and kissed me, but then pulled away to yawn again. "I'm really sorry," she said. "It's not you. I didn't get any sleep last night."

"It's fine," I said. "I'll see you tomorrow."

"Good night," she said. "I'll see you in the morning.

I went back down the hall to the elevator. I thought about going back down to the bar, but I didn't feel quite up to it. I went to my room and went out on the balcony and looked at the ocean. It was cold out on the balcony and my palms went numb when I set them on the railing. The wind was pulling sheets of mist off the water and blowing them back and forth. I knew that I should go in, because I would probably catch a cold, but I just stood there, watching the wind. But then after a while I got really cold, and so I went back inside. Once I was back inside I couldn't sit still, though. I had started thinking again about the story I'd written. I wanted to reread it and start fixing it right away. I couldn't do anything about it, though, so I went back down to the bar. I thought maybe some of our group would still be there. But when I got there, everyone had already left. I sat down at the bar and ordered a drink anyway. There was an older couple sitting next to me, and after my drink came the man started talking to me.

"Are you here with the other young folks?" he said. "I thought I saw you earlier, sitting with that group." He pointed to the table where we were all sitting. "That was you, wasn't it?"

"Yes," I said. "Did you happen to see when they left? I was actually expecting to meet them."

"It's probably been fifteen minutes," said the woman.

"No," said the man, "it hasn't been that long."

"Yes it has," she said. "I was looking at the clock because I was thinking, if all those young people are going to bed already, we certainly have no business being up." She laughed. She had a nice laugh. They were pretty old, but when she laughed she sounded much younger. If I hadn't been looking at her, I would have thought that she was my age.

"What are you all doing here?" said the man. "I mean, you're all here together, am I right?"

"We all go to school together," I said. "One of our friends got married."

"What school?" he said. I told him. "Ah," he said. Then he told me what school he went to. He was wearing his class ring. "Some good times," he said. "I'm sure you're having them now yourself. The best friends I ever had I made in college. It'll be over before you know it."

"All right," said the woman, "that's enough." She didn't say it in a mean way, though.

"What are you here for?" I said.

"It's our anniversary," said the woman. "Twenty-seven years."

"Congratulations," I said. "Let me order you some champagne." I waved to the bartender.

"Oh don't you dare," said the woman.

"We couldn't let you," said the man. "Thank you for the offer."

"All right," I said. I stopped waving to the bartender. He hadn't seen me anyway. I raised my glass towards them and said, "Well here's to you, all the same. Twenty-seven years."

We toasted and drank. After that was done there wasn't anything else to say. I sat wondering where everyone had gone and if I was the only one still awake. I said goodnight to the couple and left the bar. I was still pretty awake, but I didn't have anywhere to go. It was a horrible feeling. I knew that if I went back to my room I would lay awake forever. I pushed the button for the elevator, but then decided to take the stairs, just because it would take longer. I also thought it might make me tired. But since I was on the stairs and not the elevator I stopped on Brett's floor and went down to his room. I listened outside and I heard Brett and Julia talking and I thought probably they wanted to be alone. I was going to go back to my room, but then I heard Grant and then Rita and so I knocked and everyone got quiet and after a minute Rita opened the door. She started giggling when she saw me and everyone else did too.

"We thought you were hotel security," Brett said, "come to tell us to keep it down."

"I am," I said. "They deputized me in the lobby. You're all under arrest."

"Shut the door and have a drink," said Grant. The girl I still had not met was sitting on his knee. "Cynthia," said Grant, "be a doll and make David a drink. We don't want him to feel left out. It might make him sad."

"Grant," said Julia, "be nice."

"Lighten up," said Grant. Cynthia had moved to the table where the bottles were. "Make him a rum and coke," said Grant over his shoulder, still looking at me. "That's all that's left anyway, whether he likes it or not."

She mixed the drink and handed it to me. "I'm Cynthia, by the way," she said, shaking my hand. "I don't think we've met."

"I don't think so," I said, taking the drink and shaking her hand. "How do you know everyone?"

"I'm a friend of Rita's from back home. She invited me up for the weekend. I only live a couple hours away. I hope it isn't too strong," she said.

"No," I said, "it's perfect. Thank you."

Everyone else was listening to Paul. Paul had graduated the year before, and was still looking for a job. Paul was saying that he was thinking of going to teach English for a year in China, but his father didn't think much of that idea. His father didn't think much of most of his ideas. He always thought Paul should be doing something more prestigious. His father had a lot of confidence in him, I guess, but he had an odd way of showing it.

"That's what I'm going to do when I graduate," said Julia. "Maybe not China, but somewhere. I've already looked into it a little bit."

"Like hell you are," said Grant. "You're going to go to work for one of your dad's friends or something. There's no way in hell your parents are going to let their baby girl fly off to China to teach English to peasants."

"They're not peasants," said Julia. But I guess she didn't know who they were, because she didn't say anything else. Instead she made a big show of being upset, so that no one would ask her anything else. It was funny. Her mother had come to visit once, and I'd seen her do the same thing.

"Whoever they are," said Grant, "you're never going to find out, because you're never going to go." He looked around. "Face it," he said. "I'm never going to go, either. Neither are any of you. We're never going to be struggling artists in Soho, either. We're never going to be anything worth talking about."

"Good God," said Julia, "shut the fuck up, Grant."

After that nobody said anything. We all drank our drinks and listened to the music. I started thinking about John, and about how odd it was that he had decided to join up. He was the only one of our friends that had. It still didn't fit. I couldn't help thinking, when he told us what he was doing, that he wasn't that much like us after all. It was the same as if he'd told us that his parents were factory workers. It just wasn't how we thought of him. I started thinking that Grant was right, that we all came from too much money. Not enough to spare us any hardship, but enough to take the edge off. We were never going to really fail or really succeed. Everything was going to be blunted by a buffer of money. There would always be money. We were never going to be destitute or struggling or starving. We would have to break entirely from our parents and their money to get anywhere near an experience that was not lessened by the knowledge that we would always be protected, looked out for, and kept from anything unpleasant or dirty. It was not life at all but something else, something lived walking six inches off the ground. I had never dropped anything that could not be replaced or transgressed in a way that couldn't be corrected.

"I'm sick of rum," said Cynthia.

"That's all there is," said Grant.

"I have some gin in my room," said Julia. "I'll go and get it."

"I'll go with you," said Brett.

They left and we waited for them for a while. Then someone said that it shouldn't take as long as it was taking, and Grant snorted into his glass. Cynthia poured another round and killed the bottle. We sat drinking, and Paul talked about what it was like in the real world. Then the conversation turned back to what everyone would do with their lives. Rita said that it would all go the same way: she would marry someone and Cynthia would marry someone. It wasn't the worst of all possible fates, she said, which was true, but somehow it made me sad to hear it.

I finished my drink and said goodnight to everyone. I went outside and rode the elevator down to the lobby. The bar was closed, and so I went out and walked down the street for a while, following the ocean. There was a cluster of lights up ahead, but they were farther away than they looked. It took a long time to reach them. I thought that maybe they were just display lights, that maybe nothing was open and I would have walked all that way for nothing. Then I would have to walk all the way back. But when I got closer I found an open bar. The bar was fairly crowded, but everyone was being pretty quiet. You could still hear the television. Everyone looked tired and like they were sick of each other. I sat down at the bar and the bartender came over.

"Don't tell me," he said. "Dry martini, shaken not stirred."

"I was at a wedding," I said. I was really over-dressed. "Just a beer."

"Last call is in five," he said. "Want to order two?"

"No," I said, "one is fine."

He brought it and I sat watching the television. A roadside bomb had exploded, killing three American soldiers. It was part, the newscaster said, of an escalating trend of violence. There had already been more deaths that month than in the month before, and the month was not over. Then the waitress came over and sat down next to me. The bartender poured her two shots and she drank them without really acknowledging them. It was impressive to see. She set the two empties behind the bar and blew a kiss to the bartender.

Then the bartender gave last call, and the waitress had to carry a lot of glasses. People started to leave, and she cleared away the empties. The bartender asked me if I was watching the TV and I said no and he turned it off. I looked at the blank screen for a while. I could see my reflection, but not too well. It was kind of interesting to watch, for some reason. Then the bartender said that he could turn the television back on. I guess he had been watching me. After that I didn't look at the television anymore. I wondered if Brett and Julia had ever come back with the gin, and I started thinking that I would go back and check. Then I thought that probably they hadn't, and that everyone had probably said good night and gone to their separate rooms, and that there would be no one awake when I got back to the hotel. I wasn't sure if I wanted to rush back to the hotel or stay in the bar. At least there were people in the bar. I thought if I went back and no one was up that I could go and wake up Susan. I was drunk enough that I thought she wouldn't mind. I didn't really want to talk to Susan, though. I knew she would make me explain everything. That was the nice thing about Brett and Julia and Grant, I thought: they didn't care, and so you never had to explain yourself. Sometimes it was a relief. It was funny to think of Susan fawning over Brett. One of the most sensitive people I knew was pursuing one of the least. I didn't understand it. I figured I would ask her about it when I saw her again, or whenever I had the energy to get into it.

Then, before I knew it, everyone was gone. A big group had made so much noise leaving that I hadn't realized they were the only ones left. The waitress was clearing their glasses. I got up and started to help her. I don't really know why. I felt strange sitting there while she carried them up. But after I brought the first armload she told me she would take care of it, so I sat back down. I hadn't really drunk any of my beer, and I didn't really want it, but I guess the bartender wasn't going to kick me out until I was finished. Then the waitress and the bartender went back into the kitchen, and after a while they came out with their jackets on. The bartender asked me if I was staying at the hotel. I told him I was.

"That's where a lot of weddings stay," he said. "We can give you a ride, if you want. We're going that way."

I followed them outside and we got into his car. It was dark in the bar, but when the lights came on in the car I got a better look at them. The bartender was older, but the waitress looked like she was probably my age.

She offered me a cigarette and when I accepted she lit three in her mouth and then handed them out. I wondered where they were going, and I wanted to go with them. But instead, almost before I realized it, we pulled up in front of the hotel. I thanked them and got out. I went inside and the clerk called from across the lobby that there was no smoking and so I went back outside to finish. But once I was outside, I didn't want the cigarette anymore. I smoked it for a while anyway. Then I went back inside and rode the elevator up to Brett's floor. I heard Paul still talking so I knocked but it was only Paul and Cynthia and Rita. Grant had gone to bed. Cynthia asked me to stay.

"We found some vodka in one of Brett's suitcases," she said.

"I'll stay for one," I said.

I was still there when the sun came up. We watched it rise out of the ocean. Then we all went downstairs and ordered Bloody Marys and sat around, not speaking. Then Susan came down, and then Grant, and then Brett and Julia. We ordered them all Bloody Marys but Susan said that she didn't need it, that she would have coffee instead. She said that she was feeling fine. She certainly seemed it. I remembered that I'd wanted to talk to her, had wanted to ask her what she found so fascinating about Brett. But in the morning with everyone sitting around hungover and me hungover too it seemed like a stupid idea, and that after all I really didn't care that much. Then we started talking about the newlyweds.

"It's so odd to think that they're married," said Rita. "I still think of them as dating. I guess somehow I always thought they would just be a couple. Not that they would be one of those couples that never got married, but just a couple. I guess that doesn't make sense. It still seems odd. I guess it's what people do, though."

"It doesn't get any less strange," said Paul, "it just happens more often."

I wanted to tell him to shut up, but I didn't have the energy. Then the waiter came, and we ordered breakfast. But when it came, we could barely eat it. Susan was the only one with any appetite. When we paid and left most of the food was still on the table.

"They'll probably just heat it up and serve it to the next table," said Brett. Grant snorted and said he probably was right. I saw him look at Julia for a reaction, but she hadn't been paying attention.

After that Susan started complaining about how much she had to do when she got back to school. Pretty soon, Rita joined her. Before long it seemed like there were a million things to do. But I knew that Susan and Rita didn't have anything to do. Not really. None of us did. You'd never know it, listening to them. It was almost funny.

"Tell me about it," said Paul. "I have a million interviews to set up, when I get home. I shouldn't have come in the first place, really. I honestly have a million things I should be doing. I've got about a hundred résumés that should already be in the mail. Don't even get me started."

No one seemed interested in getting him started. Susan and Rita kept on like they hadn't heard him. No one could relate to his problems. I thought again about John, and about how comforting it must be to receive orders. That was the appeal of the soldier's life, I thought. You made one decision that included all of the others you would ever make. You never had to worry about who to send a résumé to or what color tie to wear to an interview. It was never a question of what classes you would take or what career you would pursue or where you would live. They told you what to do and where to live so you went. It was very simple. I knew that I had nothing to do when I got back to school. I would unpack and then sit around my room, and the day would slowly go down into evening. Then night would come, and everyone would be busy finishing things for the next morning. Then sleep and then waking, and then long hours of nothing followed by nothing, and an inevitable sort of life to follow, until I had replaced my father and it was no longer myself but now my son who stood to face the world. It didn't seem so much tragic as it seemed superfluous.

We went outside to look at the ocean. Susan took my arm. She did it so Brett could see.

"David and I had the loveliest walk along the beach last night," she said. "We went all the way down to those rocks." She pointed, but no one was looking at her. "Then we walked all the way back. The ocean is so beautiful at night. I wish we'd gone swimming."

"That water is probably sixty degrees," said Paul. "You'd probably have gone numb as soon as you hit the water, and drowned."

"God, Paul," said Julia. "You've got a razor wit, anyone ever tell you that? I mean you're a real charming sort of guy. I can see why everyone wants to hire you."

We started walking, and Paul kept up with us. Susan was with me and Rita was with Grant and Cynthia with them and Julia was with Brett. Paul didn't have anyone to walk with. It became something more, after what Julia said. It became like nobody wanted him there. It was unpleasant to watch, because Paul wasn't really a bad guy. All the same, I felt a sudden and acute repulsion towards him. Everyone else seemed to feel it, too. After a while he stopped, and I looked back and saw him staring out over the ocean. He did it with the same demeanor he'd used earlier when he said that marriages did not get less strange, just more common. It was a kind of exaggerated worldliness. It was obvious that he was still one of us, then, and I felt sorry that circumstances made it seem like he was not. Standing on the beach staring out at the ocean as we walked away, he was the loneliest person I had ever seen. Then he waved, and I saw him call goodbye, but the wind had picked up and so we didn't hear him, and I was the only one who noticed. I waved back, but he had already turned toward the hotel and so he didn't see me wave. I wanted to chase after him, to somehow make up for how cold we had all been. It wasn't his fault, really. His life was the truth that put the lie to our play-lives, and so we hated him for it. It didn't seem fair. But then I turned and kept walking with everyone. When I looked back again Paul was far down the beach. Then I saw him turn up towards the hotel.

One of the girls shrieked and I turned back. Rita had her shoes off, and was walking down where the tide came in. The waves splashed over her feet and left rings of foam around her ankles. Other people in other parts of the world were starving, being blown up, being systematically executed. There was no justification for us except that we were, and wouldn't negate our own existence by asserting its frivolity.

Nor would we change, nor did we have the strength to change. Nor did it matter in the least. I watched the foam bubbles slowly bursting on Rita's legs and thought how wonderful it was to be young, to be young and free and well-off, and how funny it was that we were all so fundamentally unhappy. I knew that I didn't have any real problems, that to call my problems problems was to cheapen the idea of problems itself. I stopped and took off my shoes and socks and rolled up my pants to my knees and joined Rita in the waves. I had thought that if I joined in, everyone else would too. But they just stood there, watching us from the dry sand higher up.

Then Julia said that she didn't feel well, and Cynthia didn't either, and everyone started back. Rita put her shoes back on and hurried to catch them. She was very clever about it. She stood at the edge where the wave would just reach her, and dipped her foot in as the wave came in to wash away the sand. Then she put on her shoe as the wave went out, and switched so that the foot with the shoe would stay dry while she rinsed the other.

I had socks, and so it was more difficult. I crossed the beach and found a clump of grass to sit down on while I waited for my feet to dry. Then I brushed away most of the sand and put my shoes and socks back on. When I stood up to roll down my pant legs I could see them all, far out ahead of me. I started running after them, but found that I could not run fast enough to escape the feeling that I would never catch them.

*Later, They Fought
Over the Most Trivial Things*

Later, they fought over the most trivial things. He would say that he was going out, she would demand to know where, and a battle would ensue that would last longer, he always realized later, than it would have taken in the first place, just going out and not telling her. She was not jealous, but felt abandoned when he left; he was neither unfaithful nor averse to her joining him, but only resentful of being made to always give an account of himself and his actions. There's no thoughtlessness, he would say. You make everything I do into evidence! It's exhausting, to not be allowed unintentional behavior. To which she would reply that there was, of course, no unintentional behavior: that he, having been a student in the same Introduction to Psychology course which she herself took two years after him should know well enough that the subconscious, though obfuscated and cryptic, was author of all so-called unintentional action.

To this he had no reply: the only reply would have been to tell her that, after all, she was not a doctor, and thus could hardly be considered qualified to make any such statements about his state of mind, or draw any such conclusions. But an assertion like this would have been poorly received, would have been considered extremely mean-spirited, and would doubtless have prompted yet another round of her uninformed and hackneyed analysis. Why, after all, did he feel it necessary to cut her down in this fashion? It was true that she was not a doctor, but she was happy as a nurse. He could ask her mother, if he did not believe her: she had wanted to be a nurse ever since she was young. His protestations

- that this wasn't even what he was talking about - would be lost in the overwhelming wave of her hurt (not that what he had said had hurt her, of course, but that according to her he had *said it to hurt her*). So instead he said nothing, and nodded, a reply that was by now a reflex disconnected from its connotations, and no longer implied agreement or accord. He simply nodded - like Pavlov's dog, he thought to himself -because it was the only thing that ever stopped her.

＊

But then there were plenty of other times, insignificant times, when the amorphous *oneness* of their union seemed irrefutable and beyond any danger of destruction or dissolution. The perfect harmony of their behaviors, if not their words or even their (he was so tired of the word) *feelings*, formed an impregnable bulwark which not even their combined efforts could tear down. We've become some sort of mythological two-headed monster, he would say, and now neither of us can survive without the other, and our feelings about the matter are entirely beside the point.

To this his single friends would shake their heads and advise him that this was not the description of a healthy or a functional relationship, that they had grown *co-dependent* (he could never suppress a smile at the distain in their voices when they said this word; what was the point of a relationship, he always thought in silent reply, if not co-dependency?), that he should move out, that he should ask her to move out, and, always, that he would thank them in the end for giving him this advice.

But his married friends only nodded and shrugged, and asked him if he thought he would be happier with someone else, and did he really think that he would find someone better, someone who knew him better, someone who loved him more? To these points he no longer gave opposition: all arguments about the Cardinal Sin of wasted possibility, the existential concerns regarding lives chosen or forsaken, seemed pretentious and beside the point in the face of such simple, sensible logic. In these moments, facing these friends, the argument at the core of *what could be* seemed easily and wholly over-whelmed by the case for *what was*: the possible future lives he imagined for himself, upon closer inspection, seemed ridiculous and fantastic, and all vacillation on the point for their sake seemed the stuff of profound immaturity. He would leave these conversations imbued with a tranquil and seemingly imperturbable certainty, a sense that the life he was living was superior not only to all immediate potential others but indeed to all others (that he alone lived in the traveling spotlight of the universe's benevolent regard), in which he would bask for no less than two but usually no more than five days, be-fore all invariably crumbled and he was left again with his nagging and implacable doubts.

✳

Yes, she would say, but do you love me *enough*? To which he could only reply, enough for what?

❋

Her friends had their own ideas.

He doesn't make you happy, they would say. What are you doing? You're twenty-six. Is he going to ask you? Do you want him to ask you? Do you want to have children with this person? You don't want to wait too long, they would say. You should really think about what you're doing, they would say.

One weekend they organized a trip to surprise her. Four friends picked her up from work and drove with her three hours to the border of the next state. In the call she made home to him she sounded, her friends agreed, too apologetic, and one of them took the phone from her and declared (to him, but loud enough to elicit cheers and hoots from the others in the car) that she was off limits that weekend, that no *man* was going to stop their fun. At the casino and in the hotel room she participated half-heartedly, attempting to be amicable in the name of the considerable effort these friends had undertaken on her behalf, and resisting openly only with protests that she worked too hard for her money to throw it away gambling.

There were, however, plenty of other things to do.

They stayed in the room, playing music through the cheap radio and drinking cocktails that they made themselves. The plan was to go to one of the shows playing that night, but no one could agree which one. They took turns in the bathroom mirror, getting ready. Finally, without a plan, they left, walking carefully in tight skirts and high heels, giggling at their reflection in the elevator's mirrored door. She thought of calling him but worried about slurring her words, or being caught by one of her friends. Down in the bar they were picked up by a pair of best friends from two states away, who bought them drinks and gave them money to play the slots. After a while, and while the best friends were up at the bar, the girls began to argue amongst themselves about what to do about the men. One of the friends wanted to leave, the other three wanted to stay, though there was some dispute amongst the three as to who would go with whom. Finally one reminded the others that *she* had organized the trip, that *she* had booked the hotel room, that *she* had bought the booze and the gas. This seemed to conclude the matter, in her mind, and she walked off in the direction of the bar without a backwards glance.

It fell to the remaining four to make a plan, though none seemed interested in anything that they might do. It had been, after all, the absent friend's idea to come here, and the others' enthusiasm had stemmed largely, they explained to her, from the desire to give her the break she obviously needed. The swell of mutual emotion that this admission inspired only managed to rouse the group from its collective lethargy for a moment. Everyone was drunk, the fourth friend was nowhere to be found; the bar, though far from empty, was populated entirely by mobile, transitory groups of people moving from one room to the next, or taking a drink between games. On the elevator ride back up to the room she thanked them repeatedly, though secretly she was overwhelmed with relief that nothing now stood between her and sleep, beyond which lay only the ride back to her home and to him.

But in the morning the fourth friend was still nowhere to be found, and it was nearly two hours before she was discovered in the hotel restaurant, eating cubed fruit and drinking her second Bloody Mary. Everyone had slept poorly, having shared the room's two queen-sized beds between the four of them, and no one spoke on the drive. Finally back in the apartment she was annoyed to discover the state of her things: the four friends, packing an overnight bag for her, had gone through her closet and bureau with seemingly impious haste. It occurred to her tired and frustrated logic with sudden clarity and certainty of insight that of course their access to her things had been directly allowed by *him*, that the present condition of the room fell under the umbrella of *his* responsibility, and that the rampant disregard for the sanctity of her space could only stem from gross and grave indifference on *his* part.

*

He came home two hours late from work. She had not put her things back in order. He asked about her trip. She asked where he had been. He explained only that he had not expected her home yet. Ignoring the evaded question, she asked instead how he could have let her friends just rifle through her things. He asked what she meant. She answered only by indicating the messier places. He replied by saying that he had not been home when they came, that he had been at work, too, that he had left the key under the mat for them, and that anyway they were her friends and if she was mad at someone then she should be mad at them.

This point, though seemingly irrefutable, did little to lessen the resentment that had been building in her while she waited for him. It was, however, obvious (to him) that she had left the room in disarray so that she might accuse him with it upon his return. He, he said, had tried to help her friends do something nice for her: it wasn't his fault that they had made a mess! She replied by asking again where he had been for the two hours between when he left work and when he returned home. He replied by packing a bag, and going to sleep at a friend's house.

✳

Her friends told her she was better off. And anyway, it was obvious that he was cheating on her: why else would he storm out without answering the question? She shouldn't waste one more minute thinking about him, they said. Still, this was not what she had wanted, and she thought about him constantly. The empty apartment felt amputated, missing some essential component that the natural order dictated should be present.

Was he cheating on her? She couldn't be sure, and started driving by their friend's house after work to see if he was there with someone. On the fourth such errand, sitting on the dark street in her softly idling car, and observing (as she had on the three previous occasions) no indication of another woman, she was filled with the sense that she had made a terrible mistake, that it was all her fault, that she had lost sight of normal behavior and become driven by a baser set of infantile and immature impulses arising from low self-esteem and abandonment anxiety.

Life, the life she had been living for the nearly two weeks since his departure, seemed to her then barren and empty, and not worth living without him. Realizing this, she returned home and, after drinking a little more than a half of a bottle of white wine, called first his phone and then, when it went straight to voicemail, and despite the late hour, the house phone of the friend with whom he was staying.

The friend answered, and was at first cautious and protective, and hesitant to let her speak with him. Did she know what she had done to him? Yes, she said. Yes she knew, and yes he was right.

The conversation, when their friend finally gave him the phone, lasted for twenty minutes, and ended with the agreement that he would come to the apartment (he was under no obligation to bring his things with him, she understood if he did not want to!), and that they would talk there so that they did not keep the friend awake. The conversation, when he arrived, did not last even that long: she began to cry, said that she missed him; he cried as well, and said that he missed her. She was sorry, and so was he. He said that he loved her, and she replied the same. They made love on the couch and then again on the floor, and they finished the wine and then drank another bottle. Awake afterwards she reflected that now life seemed to have been returned to its proper course, that this was all she had ever wanted and that she was, as the saying went, happy.

✳

Their engagement came as some surprise to everyone, including her. They went out to dinner, her mind was on other things; afterwards they walked through a park near their apartment and beside the pond he explained that he had been doing a lot of thinking. It occurred to her, as he showed her the ring, that perhaps all the times he had gone out and not told her where he was going (the two hours he was absent after her return from the casino, for example) he was working a second job that he had not wanted her to know about, so that he would be able to buy her the ring: that perhaps her life had become, in some ways, like the storybook story she was thoughtlessly certain it would become when she was younger.

This was only one of the many thoughts going through her mind, and she did not stop to inquire after its veracity. Instead she held out her hand, fingers splayed, so that he might mark her acceptance. On the walk back to the car she called her parents, who in their surprise did not hide their hesitation as artfully as they might. This, however, did nothing to dampen her mood.

*

It was a confusing development for his single friends, who "had not thought that they were that serious." To this he only shrugged. His married friends seemed to understand better the nature of the gesture. The important thing, they agreed, was to commit oneself: happiness, marital or otherwise, was not found but *made*, and - questions of compatibility aside - most people and most couples were as happy as they decided to be.

This verdict, though encouraging, was spoken with the shrugging ambivalence typical of these friends' replies to such concerns, and he was left again feeling that the question he was asking was entirely beside the point: that after all marriage was not a matter of being happy. He dismissed these thoughts with private self-directed and self-produced reassurances this this *was what people did*: that the time for deciding what kind of life he wanted to live (which question he derisively referred to as the question of "what he wanted to be when he grew up," with all intended satire and irony) had passed, and that at the very least he would not go into his late twenties and then his early thirties unable or unwilling to make a start into adult life. He was, at the very least, *making the adult decision*, and the solace he found in this assessment superseded (to an increasingly lessening degree, as the day drew nearer) his concerns.

✳

He found, to his surprise, that he was observing her more closely. What was he looking for? It was obvious, even to him: he was watching for any sign of the immaturity that, by marrying her, he was attempting to sever himself from. One night, while they were watching television, she began to coo playfully at a commercial starring a number of kittens. Wewen't they just the cewtest wittle things, she wanted to know. Another night, climbing into bed with him, she asked him to tell her a story while she fell asleep. Another night, when there was a forty minute wait at their favorite restaurant, she would not speak to him while they ate at another restaurant, but instead stared poutingly into her soup. These compiled in his mind until they comprised an irrefutable body of evidence against which his private self-reassurances - that the most important thing was the act of committing - were nearly useless.

✳

Despite this, their breakup two months later propelled him into something very closely resembling despair. He returned home to find the ring sitting on the coffee table and her sitting in a chair opposite. The conversation that followed remained in his memory only as a series of disconnected moments underscored by alternating waves of lethargy and anger. He remembered, at one point, rising from the couch and kicking over the coffee table, and afterwards the two of them looking for the ring, for neither had seen where it went when it was sent flying, and thinking how absurd it all was, this bizarre act into which they seemed locked. He remembered thinking that she was right, that her view of the situation was correct, though later he could not remember exactly how she had worded her assessment, or what that assessment contained. Was it that neither was very encouraging to the other? It was something like that, but she had seemed to touch on some more profound truth in the way she had put it. He had begun to cry, though he could not have said why either then or after: it was not the rejection, he was fairly certain, nor, he thought, did it seem likely that it was the prospect of not seeing her anymore, for at that moment and throughout the conversation such seemed laughably impossible. Perhaps they were calling off the wedding, but certainly they would remain in each other's lives! How could they not? Each knew the other better than the other knew themselves.

He fell asleep on the couch, and in the morning she asked him to leave. He went to stay with another friend, and did not start looking for apartments. A week later his things arrived in boxes. He went to look for a new place, but dismissed any that he could not rent month-to-month, certain that soon she would see that she had made a mistake, and invite him to come back. After two days of looking he found and rented a small basement efficiency. He called her to see if she wanted to come see his new place, thinking that at the very least such would make her realize that consequences of her actions, for he was convinced by now that she had called off the wedding out of some adolescent impulse, some inherent misunderstanding regarding the dramatic narrative of relationships. Things did not, he imagined himself telling her, *have* to be difficult. Why turn this into something it was not? It was not, he was certain she would agree, an epic Love Story, characterized by disallowed longing and sudden reversals. She had to understand the difference between *Real Life* and whatever immature fantasy template she was drawing from.

But when he called, she didn't answer. He tried her again later, and achieved the same result. He did not own any furniture, but was hesitant to buy any until he spoke with her. He was uncertain, now, that she would invite his return. He had not heard from her in a week and a half. He slept on a blanket folded on the floor. After three nights he purchased a mattress and a couch at a thrift store, and left them side-by-side in the apartment's single room. The possibility that this small, empty place was now his home arrived with startling clarity and carried with it the full impact of what he had lost. He drank heavily and called her several times, each time receiving no answer. He became convinced that she was out on a date, that her friends (who had never liked him, he was certain) had set her up with someone the moment he was out of the apartment. Later and very drunk, he became convinced that he would find them if he went looking, and stumbled out into the street where he was almost struck by a passing car. The excitement of this caused him to be sick, and convinced him that he should go home. He eschewed both couch and mattress and slept instead on the bathroom floor, uncertain whether he would be sick again, a decision for which he was later grateful.

✽

How could she explain it? It was too easy for them to fall into a way of being that wasn't good for either of them. She was certain that he understood what she was talking about. It was not enough for the relationship to be comfortable and familiar: comfortable and familiar could become a trap!

And so on, and so on. He crumpled the letter and threw it away, then pulled it from the trash and reread it. Then he folded it but, having no table to desk, he had nowhere to put it.

✽

His friends empathized to varying degrees. His single friends encouraged him to think about the future and to remember, if anything, how unhappy she had made him. His married friends, having a somewhat less severe view, commiserated without offering advice. For three months he was transported with grief and frustration. If only she would talk to him, he was certain that they could work things out. Then life could go back to the way it was supposed to be. She had sent a letter, but what could he do with a letter? He couldn't talk to a letter!

Had they seen her? How had she looked? Who was she with? Was she seeing anyone? To these questions his friends answered truthfully, to varying degrees.

＊

He found another apartment, and moved out of the efficiency. He bought furniture. He stopped drinking and joined a new gym. He allowed himself to be set up, and went out on dates. He found himself thinking about her, but now her memory was colored by the memory of the months after their breakup, and he could hardly think of one without the other. He found that he looked forward to returning home at the end of the day, and that his home no longer seemed empty without her. He began dating one of the girls he had been set up with. He was surprised one morning to realize that their wedding, had it occurred, would have been that afternoon. The initial sadness this realization produced was almost instantly superseded by its strangeness: his life was so drastically different from what it had been, and it seemed impossible that, in another life, in another universe, he would at this very moment be preparing to marry her. It was only, in fact, with some effort that he was able to again produce in his mind an image of her as his wife, which struck him as odd, as less than a year earlier this image had never been far from this thoughts.

He had little time to contemplate this: he was running late for work, and was meeting some friends after for a drink. Then the girl he was dating was coming over for dinner. It seemed sad and strange that life moved on, that the importance of something that once seemed vital and immutable and without which his life would collapse could be so easily dissolved in so short a time. It seemed sad and strange that, in the final estimation, the important things in his life were not so important after all, not even to him.

*The Distinction of the Mature and the
Horror of the Naïve*
or
"¿Comprende Más Tequila?"

She came down to the lobby bar. The bartender spotted her as she exited the elevator and he had her drink half-made when she arrived. She'd ordered the same thing every night and sometimes during the day since Friday midday. Today was Tuesday. The bartender thought that that could not be right. Had he worked through the weekend, every day since Friday? He counted the days back over in his mind. It was so hard to tell: the days were all the same. That was one thing about a hotel bar, he thought. It was easy to get used to changing faces. There were never any regulars. Perhaps that was why he enjoyed making her drink before she arrived, when he saw her coming. That way he could pretend that they shared something. Shared what? A ritual, he thought. In the past five days they had come to share a ritual. That had to mean something.

The bartender spoke English, but was happy to pretend that he did not. He did not want to speak to the people who came into the lobby bar. In the beginning he'd assumed that a friendly bartender was tipped better, and so had talked to everyone. That was before he knew about people - or at least about Americans - and knew that when they felt ignorant or ridiculous they always tried to make it better with money. So he had stopped speaking to everyone when he realized that there was no profit in being a friendly bartender, and instead he let them believe that he spoke no English whatsoever, and let them fumble through insultingly bad Spanish before resigning themselves to silent patronage.

He stopped speaking to them also when it became clear that they had no interest in listening to him. It was a hard realization, and he had arrived at it with the sense that he was growing into maturity: that the mark of maturity was the acceptance of unpleasant truths about one's self and one's position in life. If he was to be the bartender then that was all there was to it. He could not imagine anything else. All of the older employees had started at the hotel at the same age as him. He washed dishes in the kitchen and then cleaned rooms and then, for the past six months, worked behind the bar. Probably he would stay at the bar and then later manage the night shift and then maybe something else. It was a job that his friends envied. It would not make for an epic life, an interesting life, a great life, but it was a good job, and he knew that he would not leave it because he was the bartender and that was all there was to it.

This was the unpleasant truth he had accepted. This gave him the sense that he knew a lot about life and that it was a shame that no one listened to him, because he spoke English very well, and had plenty to say. *Yes*, he thought: *it is a shame that no one listens, because really I have quite a bit to say. I know more about life and about these people than they know about themselves. I have been watching them very closely for almost three years. It will be three years in July. They could learn a lot, listening to me.*

And anyway it was easier to say *margarita, si, cervesa, si,* and listen to them complain about each other. Yes: that was something he would have told them, if they listened. Americans all brought their troubles with them. Where they were didn't make any difference. All their money didn't buy them anything worth having if they came here to forget, and couldn't. No: that was not all true. It bought them beer and it bought them rum and it bought them margaritas. It bought them margaritas so they could sit and tell themselves that they were having a real Mexican time, a *tiempo auténtico. My god*, he thought, *the things they could learn from me, if they would only listen.*

She had not asked him if he spoke English, and so he was spared the burden of lying to her. *Spared.* That was funny. Of course he thought nonchalantly about lying until he was allowed not to. Then it became obvious how he felt about it. What could he do? He had been raised not to lie and did not like lying, especially for the sake of economics. Wasn't that why he told himself that they did not listen anyway: to ease his own guilt about lying to them? It was funny. His hopeless, predictable, Catholic guilt. He again had the sense that he was facing a hard truth about himself, and that the ability to face such truths was a mark of his having passed from boyhood into maturity. But then he caught sight of his own smooth cheeks in the mirror glass behind the bottles, and he laughed. Yes, that was the face of maturity! He arranged the bottles, bringing them forward to sit along the shelf's edge, watching his reflection between them. It was a hopelessly juvenile face. He did not even look his own age.

The older man at the bar's end called for another drink. The bartender mixed it and brought it and the older man asked him to make one for her as well. The bartender did not want to and thought of pretending that he had not understood. But then he mixed the drink and set it in front of her. When she looked at him he pointed, indicating the older man. The older man waved and she stood and overturned the drink into the basin on the other side of the bar. The bartender had to move quickly to avoid getting any on him. Nevertheless, it made him exceedingly happy. He took the empty glass from her with a smile that she did not seem to notice. He went into the back to get more bottles.

When he came back some rearrangements had been made.

"You didn't have to do that," the older man was saying. "If you didn't want it, you could have sent it back to me. I'm not a rich man." He laughed and raised his glass, moving his fingers slightly so that his rings would catch the light. If she noticed she did not let on. Because of this the bartender felt extremely proud of her.

"I know," said the older man, striking his forehead with his palm in pantomime of realization. "Of course! I ordered you the wrong drink. I must have told this bartender to make you another of what *I* was having, instead of another of what *you* were having. Will you give a broken old man the chance to make it up to you?"

"You're not so old," she said, looking him over. "And you don't look very broken. Are you broken?"

"Not very much," he said, "and nowhere important."

"I guess that was pretty rude of me," she said, "pouring out your gift like that."

He grinned and said, "I'm sure we can figure out some way for you to make it up to me."

"Well," she said, "you can buy me another, if it would make you feel better."

"It would," he said. "You want to know what would make me feel even better than that?"

"I'm not sure I want you feeling any better than buying me a drink is going to make you feel."

"I wouldn't be so quick to come to any conclusions about that," he said. "I have a tendency to get very generous when I feel better." He raised what was left of his drink, again moving the fingers with the rings. "Remember what I said," he said, "about not being a rich man?" He grinned at her through the glass. "I was lying."

The bartender, who had been listening to their conversation, was leaning toward them across the bar. The older man turned to order and sat back, surprised at how close the bartender had come. The girl had no discernible reaction to this whatsoever.

"Geez buddy," said the older man.

"*¿Un otro?*" said the bartender.

"*Si,*" said the older man. "And one for the lady. And how about you make them down there." He pointed to the other end of the bar.

The bartender gave him a blank expression, looked in the direction he was pointing, then mixed their drinks exactly where he stood. The girl excused herself. There were no bathrooms in the bar. The closest ones were on the other side of the lobby, near the elevators. The older man watched her retreating reflection in the mirror behind the bottles. From where he stood, facing the lobby, the bartender could watch her directly. He watched her until she had disappeared behind the closing door.

"*Una chica muy bonita,*" said the bartender. He was mixing the older man's drink. Her margarita was finished, but he had it behind the bar so that he could set it in front of her when she returned. "*Como un sueño. ¡Mi corazón, mi corazón!*" He laughed, enjoying the older man's obvious discomfort.

"*Muy bonita, si,*" said the older man suddenly, and with what the bartender told himself was the worst accent he'd ever heard. "I'll tell you all about it, *hombre.*" He removed ten dollars from his billfold and held it out to the bartender. "This is for you," he said. "*Para ti,* if you put *más tequila* in *este margarita. ¿Comprende más tequila?*"

The bartender smiled and took the bill from the older man. She was coming back across the lobby, and the bartender did nothing at all but watch her. The older man repeated his instructions, but then noticed her reflection and so fell silent. The bartender set her drink on the bar as she approached. It was his favorite moment of the day. It had been his favorite moment of every day for the past five days.

"Whatever you did in there," said the older man, looking her over, "I approve."

"I took a piss," she said. The salted rim of the glass was between her teeth.

"I approve of that, too," said the older man.

"I'm so glad."

"I'm glad that you're glad." He raised his glass and sat waiting for her to touch hers to his. When it became clear that he could wait for a long time she acquiesced.

"To new friends in exotic locations," he said. "And to the best highball made by the dumbest Mexican I've ever met." He laughed and drank.

He knew that he was drunk, now: knew that he had been drunk before he drank from the fresh drink, knew it because he had called the bartender a dumb Mexican without meaning it and without thinking about it first. He had reached that point where he could feel it slipping away but knew that he could do nothing to bring it back, could do nothing because he was drunk and could not think straight, and would have to be very careful to finish out the evening without making things any worse. This was going to be a great challenge, because once things went bad they always got worse, and he would only get more ridiculous and more earnest and then he would be done for. If he could hold out until he grew more sober there was still a chance but of course now he'd had another one on top of the drunk that he was already, and as it was he was still only coming into the beginning of that drunk. He looked at himself in the mirror behind the bar between the bottles and thought, *You are a ridiculous man. You are a sad, pathetic man. Worse than that, you are old. That is the only unforgivable sin and you have committed it. There's no hiding it now. You're a cat burping bird feathers.* He ran his hands over hair, seeing his sunburned scalp through the thinning gray. *Yes,* he thought, *you are drunk and now that you are drunk you see the sad truth about yourself. You see the sad, hard truth. If that isn't maturity then I don't know what is. Your wives all told you to grow up and now you have. Congratulations. You make a fine debutante.* He looked at his reflection again and laughed. Then he stood up.

"Please bill this all to my room," he said very carefully. "Number one hundred thirty-six. *Número uno tres seis.*" He smiled at the girl who, for the first time all evening, was watching him with unwavering attention. "Goodnight, *bonita,*" he said. "Sleep well. Have another on me."

He felt unsteady on his feet. But then he found that he was moving across the lobby with quick, light steps, walking as though he was not walking at all but floating. *Yes,* he thought, *I've done a long graceful glide to the elevators and that is the best I can hope for, for her to see me make a long and graceful and dignified exit, and maybe that is enough after all and better, too, because you always forget what happens in the dark but now you'll always have this moment, this graceful and dignified exit. You'll remember this always.* But he knew it was very likely that he would not remember it - not the next morning, nor ever - that he would wake up in bed with no recollection of how he'd made it from the bar to his room. He felt a pang of nostalgia for this moment, this moment that was occurring, this beautiful moment that he knew he would not remember. But then his thoughts wandered, and he found that he was unable to remember what it was, exactly, that had inspired his nostalgia.

He had been married three times, with all three ending without warning and all in the same way. It was almost funny. With each he had told himself that their problems were the problems that always came between men and women, that they were common problems and not the final problems, and so he was surprised each time when it was these problems that were cited in final letters and telephone messages, in meetings with lawyers and court documents. He considered it a mark to his credit that he had thought each of his marriages too well-founded to be threatened by such inconsequential misunderstandings, and declared it a point of pride that he had been blindsided by each, that his only sin was having had too much faith in the women he'd made his wives. This pride was passing and short-lived, and of little comfort. Privately he knew that he had been brought to this by his own missteps, knew that, if he'd managed to learn them, the lessons of the first could have helped him save the second, and the lessons of the first and second combined might have saved the third. Perhaps, he told himself, it was no good anyway: he'd realized with the first that he was no good as a husband, and had managed to fool himself that it was not true when the time came to marry the others. But there it was. He was no good as a husband. The irony was that he could not live without a wife. It was funny. The times when he was not married he lived in hotels, dependent on maids. He'd been at this hotel three weeks, and knew all of the maids by name.

He went into his room and then out through the sliding door and onto the balcony overlooking the beach and the ocean. He could hear the waves on the shore and in between the waves he could hear voices. He listened for a long time, trying to make out what they were saying. The voices came closer and then seemed to be coming from directly beneath his room. He heard a boy saying something in Spanish and a girl laughing, and another boy asked in English what the other boy had said. He did not sound unfriendly, only curious. Then they moved away and everything but the sound of their voices was lost against the ocean noise. He tried for a long time to listen, but could not hear any more words. Then he heard the girl laugh. Then the sound disappeared entirely and there was only the ocean.

He knew that he was coming into the drunk in earnest, now, coming into it with a suddenness he found familiar and not altogether unpleasant. It would come on like growing tired, and he would feel like he could not keep his eyes open any longer, and then he would be asleep. It was so much easier than laying in bed, waiting to sleep. He'd done that plenty, too, and it never got him anywhere.

He went back inside, but left the balcony door open behind him. He was glad that the girl from the lobby bar had not come back with him, glad that he could be there alone in the dark with the ocean noise and the feeling that he could not keep his eyes open. Having her there would have ruined it. He knew that there was no point in denying it, to himself or anyone else: he was certainly an old man, if being here alone, allowed to sleep, was what he preferred. He had expected this realization to be harder than it was. He wondered, briefly, why he had been fighting it so passionately, and for so long. But then he felt that he was drifting, and through the sleep haze thought he heard the voices back beneath his room, and the girl's laughter. But then he was asleep, and the laughter faded into the sound of the waves and the wind through the palm boughs outside.

Downstairs the girl had ordered another drink on his tab. She was the only one left in the bar. The bartender had used the last of the lime, and was squeezing more into a bottle for the next day's margaritas, and thinking of what he should say to her.. But before he said anything the late shift came on at the lobby desk, and the evening clerks came into the bar. They were sweating and tired. They said hello to the bartender and then did not say anything else. They watched their beer as they drank it. One wore his hair tied back and when he undid the binding and let it down it hung damp and stringy around his face. The other made a kissing noise at him and the clerk whose hair hung down scowled. That was the end of it. The bartender went back to squeezing the limes, and hoped that the clerks would leave so that he could be alone with her again. Then the two clerks left.

The bartender shucked the rinds into the trash and screwed the top on the bottle.

She'd thought about having another before the bar closed, but thought better of it when she saw what trouble it was to get the lime juice. It was so unlike her. On any other night she would have ordered two more, for this same reason. Perhaps she was growing up. *No*, she thought, *that isn't it.*

"Do you speak English?" she said.

"A little," he said. He was wiping down the place where he had cut the limes.

"Do you like working here?"

"It's all right," he said. "It's a good job. All my friends tell me how lucky I am, so I guess I like it." He looked at her glass. "Do you want another one?" he said. "I was supposed to give last call five minutes ago, but I don't mind. And anyway there's no one else here."

"Yes," she said. "Only no, never mind. I saw how much trouble it was with the limes. I don't want to put you through it just for one drink. I can just as easily have something else. I'm not cruel."

"Please," he said. "If you would like another I would be happy to make you another. It would be my pleasure." He took another glass from the shelf behind the bar and salted the rim. "A beautiful margarita for a beautiful girl."

"You speak English very well," she said.

"*Gracias*." He was putting the ice and the lime and the tequila together in the shaker. She had understood that his saying "Thank you" in Spanish was a joke, and she laughed. She could not hear her own laughter over the noise from the ice in the shaker but she was certain that he had seen her and that was almost the same thing.

"How old are you?" she asked when the shaker stopped.

"Seventeen," he said. "I will be eighteen at the end of this month. How old are you?" He poured the drink into the glass and set it in front of her.

"Nineteen." She took a drink. "Are all margaritas better in Mexico, or just yours?"

"Just mine." He blushed and began to rinse the shaker. "I make the best margaritas in Mexico. You can ask anybody." He smiled and when she laughed at the joke he laughed too. "No," he said, "that's not true. That's a lie." He was still laughing. "I only make them good for my friends."

"Are we friends now?"

"Why not?" he said. "Do you already have too many friends?"

She laughed and drank again. "All right," she said, "we're friends."

She knew that she had him, now: knew that it could go forward simply and that it was all at her discretion, knew that whatever she chose to do he would take it for what it was and not question it. *I should have lived in a machismo country,* she thought. *Things are so much simpler. It's always simpler when things are stated at the outset. Things get so maddeningly confused when they pretend that they don't want what they want. That is not much of an excuse because they all want that regardless, and it's easy enough to predict and in any case has not proved to be much of an obstacle. Still, when it is stated at the outset there is nothing to wonder about anymore. It is the wondering that makes it insufferable. These guilty Catholics with their reactionary machismo. There's no one like them at Bard. All of those boys with their self-doubt and their hesitation. They're all so much goddamned work. None of them know what this bartender knows, without having been taught anything. It's all instinct. Everything worth knowing comes from instinct and if you don't have it then you will never have it. It's no use going to school. It's funny. All those boys who don't know how to make a first move and they're learning Chaucer and Shakespeare and Kant. If that isn't a indictment of the race then I don't know what is.*

It was clear to her then that if she was thinking like this she must be drunk, and that between the wine at dinner and the beer before, and the margaritas here, she very likely was. It occurred to her then that the same must be obvious to him, and she knew that she could say anything.

She'd come to Mexico alone with the vague idea that she would fall in among vacationers her own age: that the beach and the pool and the bar would be crowded with others like herself fleeing New England Christmases and insufferable families. Instead, she'd spent five days walking from her room to the beach and back, to the bar and back, to the resort's restaurants and back, and had seen no one she wanted to talk to or know. It had been an overwhelming disappointment, and she regretted having wasted her Christmas present asking for the trip. By the second day she had begun to think of all that she might have received, and her family no longer seemed so insufferable. It seemed, in fact, that they might have been easily endured for the sake of this bag that she wanted more than anything, or the car they had been talking about buying her. It hardly seemed fair. After all: she had not received what she'd asked for. She wondered if there was some way to convey this to her parents.

"Put this one on my friend's tab," she said. And then, "not you. I mean," she pointed to the now empty bar-stool, "my other friend. *Número whatever whatever whatever.*" She laughed and slapped the bar with her open palm.

"I put the others on his," the bartender said, coming over. "That one was a gift."

"A gift?"

"For you." He was smiling, and she smiled back at him without realizing it.

"You're a cute kid," she said in a tone that was meant to make up for the smile she had not intended. "I know what you're thinking," she said in a sing-song voice.

"What am I thinking?"

She laughed and drank. More got in her mouth than she expected and it made her head hurt from the cold. She wondered if she had made a face when it began to hurt, even though she had intended not to. She hoped that she had not but she could not remember, and so could not be certain. In any case the bartender was still smiling.

"I've been here for five days," she said suddenly, "and I haven't seen one shark."

"You want to see sharks?"

"I was told that I could see sharks."

"Have you been out very far into the ocean?"

"No," she said. "I've been looking from shore. I haven't seen any fins."

"It is not so common to see fins," he said. "I've lived here all my life, and I've only seen them a couple of times. Really it is not so common."

"I've been here for five days," she said again. "I'm leaving tomorrow. Will I see sharks tomorrow? Can you make them come to shore, so I can see them?" She laughed again. Her glass was empty, and she slid it to him. He took it and set it in the basin behind the bar without moving from where he was standing.

"Perhaps if you do not see any sharks tomorrow you will have to come back and visit me," he said, "now that we are friends." Then he said, "In Spanish we call shark *tiburón*."

"Tiburón," she said.

"Tiburón," he repeated, nodding. "Very good. You sound just like you were born here."

"Tiburón," she said again, imitating his accent. She had intended to tease him, but it came out sounding unkind. She was relieved to see that he had not stopped smiling. "I've been ordering drinks from you for five days," she said, "wishing that you spoke English. Now I

find out that you do and I barely have a chance to talk to you." She was suddenly overwhelmed by the tragedy of this. She reached out to touch his arm, but was not looking and missed. She got it on the second try.

"It has been nice to see you every day," he said. "It has been nice to see a friendly face."

"I have a friendly face?"

"You have a friendly face."

"I bet that's what you say to all the drunk American girls."

"I only say it to some American girls."

She thought *that's it then, isn't it. Of course that's it. You shouldn't have asked if you didn't want to know the answer. Anyway he is joking or he is pretending that he is joking and anyway what does it matter if he is joking because you are not going to see him ever again and if he is using you then it is only to the same degree that you are using him. And it doesn't matter because you know what he is doing and you can see it and you are not blinded by it. If he is playing on what he imagines is you naivety then let him and the cleverer game is to let him believe that he is doing it. What does it matter that all the charm has gone out of it? And anyway aren't you funny. You want to be able to take them but don't want to be taken. You want to use them without feeling used. Well you certainly know what you want. Good luck trying to get it.* She touched his arm again, careful this time to get it on the first try.

"I have," she said, "the most beautiful view of the ocean from my room. I wonder if there are any sharks

out now. I could sit on my balcony and watch for them."
He did not say anything. "Of course it might get lonely,"
she said. "Do you want to come and look for sharks with
me?"

He hesitated, then said, "I have to finish up here.
Maybe after."

"Sure," she said, although she understood from this
that he was not coming. "Sure. Ok. Just knock. I'll be
up."

She got up carefully and left the bar. Walking across
the lobby she felt obvious and ridiculous, and this feeling (and the feeling that her last chance to redeem the
trip had come and gone, that the five days in their total-
ity were now finally nothing but a prolonged disappointment) suddenly overwhelmed her and filled her
eyes with tears.

But she knew that they were not real tears, that it
was only that she was drunk, and for a moment the
world had seemed worthless and empty, and that nothing
could make her feel better ever again. But she knew that
this was not true: that at this time tomorrow she would
be back home, and then, shortly after, back at school,
heading on through her life, while the bartender remained here, serving drinks to American girls with his
sad, affected charm and growing older. She was certain
that he was watching her and she thought, *at least I have
this. At least I have this long, graceful exit and he will
know that I walking out of his life. And in any case I
probably won't remember how it happened, there'll just
be a feeling in the morning. But I won't see him any-*

more, and I'll never get reminded, and the feeling will fade. Yes, she thought, *that is some comfort.*

She turned to wave when she reached the elevators, but found that he had moved from his place behind the bar, and she could no longer see him. She felt ridiculous for having invited him to her room and ridiculous for her self-conscious exit because he had not been watching and didn't care at all that she was leaving. She thought she would wave when he returned, but the elevator arrived before he did, and so she got on. She pressed the button for the fourth floor, but changed her mind and pressed the button for the second. She got off and walked down the hall to room one hundred and thirty-six, and knocked. She waited for a long time, knocking again every minute or so with the heel of her hand. Eventually the door opened, and there was some brief discussion and explanation. Then she went inside and the door closed behind her.

Downstairs the bartender had returned and was washing her glass. He could see the clear imprint of her lips on the rim. The edge where her mouth had touched was bare of salt. The glass seemed to hold connotations of poignant tragedy and he felt a sudden longing to turn away, to wash the glass without looking at it and to never think of it again. Instead he looked at the glass until the feeling faded, until he no longer felt the tragedy but only knew it, until he felt indifferent to his own regret.

Again he had the sense that he was passing from boyhood into maturity, that the willingness and ability to behold such things was the mark of a mature man. He finished washing the glass and set it on the shelf. When he came in again, he knew, it would be mixed in with the other glasses, and he would be unable to tell which it had been. He was glad. The pain he felt was the pain of his illusion dying and he was glad to see it die. Dead illusions, after all, were the distinction of the mature and the horror of the naïve. He was happy to find that he felt less horror than he felt other things.

Yes, he thought, *I am becoming mature. There is nothing else in life but being mature and being beyond yearning and beyond dissatisfaction and disappointment. It is a good job and besides three years is not so long. Not in the stretch of things. Not in the history of the hotel nor of Mexico nor of the ocean nor of the earth. Three years is nothing. And even if I am here longer it is not so bad because what is five years or eight years or ten? Just the same as three, held up against the ocean.*

And anyway it is better that she turned out to be a disappointment. It was not that you were scared, it was only that you did not want her anymore after the way she talked about the sharks and it was obvious and all of the charm had gone out of it. And anyway what would have happened would have been worth less than five beautiful days, making her drinks and then having them ready when she arrived. It would not have been a culmination but rather a negation.

He thought this and then laughed, because he knew that he was only justifying his own cowardice. It had been a wonderful night for facing unpleasant truths. He had aged ten years without aging a day. He was a coward when it came to women. Had he followed her to her room, he would have had no idea what to do. So he stood behind the bar, telling himself he knew something about what it would have been worth. That was funny. He had tried to skip experience and go right to wisdom. If that wasn't an indication of his immaturity he did not know what was. But it hardly mattered now: even if he changed his mind she had not told him her room number, and so it was out of his hands. But of course he knew that it was written on all of her receipts for the last five days. All he had to do was go into the drawer in the office and look.

He turned out the lights and left the bar. He walked through the double doors leading off the far side of the lobby and down the beach to stand and stare at the ocean. The moon hung low over the water, and it and its reflection seemed to him like two eyes, watching him as the proud and beautiful tragedy of his life played itself out beneath them.

Out beneath the waves sharks swam in amongst the colorful species of fish that had populated the reefs along the shore for hundreds of thousands of years. The reef flourished and teemed with life, and the old grew weak and slowed. Eventually one ceased its movements and sank slowly toward the dense blackness along the ocean's floor. Soon it was joined by others, while high above in the shallows the coming generations sported and ate and grew. Soon these too grew old, and fell from life, and others came of age, and the sun traced its arc across the surface above, and decades and centuries passed and the bartender, the girl, and the older man died and were mourned over and were forgotten, and the hotel was razed, and eventually the whole proud and ridiculous history of human endeavors had ceased and there remained only the timeless and teeming animal life, slipping from generation to generation.

The boy, standing on the shore, did not know any of this. To him, the night's events had transpired beneath the moon's watchful eyes, awash in its bittersweet glow: the planets had ceased their orbiting to observe what had occurred. He had no way of knowing, being only seventeen, that soon he too would be old, that the astonished realization that three years had passed would be nothing compared to the feeling that, after all, a life was not so long, not in the stretch of things, not compared to the ocean or the earth. He wondered, briefly, if the evening's events would come to number among his life's great regrets, if the girl he had not pursued would haunt him, if he would always wonder. He felt certain that it would. Anticipating the history of regret that lay before him was among the most beautiful feelings he had ever known. It would not be until much later that he would come to see the ridiculousness of this speculation: come to see that of course at seventeen he'd had no regrets, having seen too little of life to know the import of anything, nor what significance things would come to hold. It would be then, too, that he would laugh at his years of self-ascribed maturity, laugh at his self-lauding claims, laugh because they were hopelessly inaccurate and beyond that, because they were juvenile in the worst possible sense. And he would know then that he was mature, that maturity truly was the ability to face the hard truths about oneself, that he really knew a great deal about life, and had plenty to say. But of course no one listened to him: he was the bartender, and no one listened to the bartender.

But this realization was still a long way off. He walked back up the beach, certain he'd heard someone calling his name, expecting that the earlier shift had returned for another drink before the long walk home. But when he reached the lobby the bar was empty, and the night clerks had not called him.

A family had arrived while he was outside, and the children were asleep on the chairs that ringed the lobby's central column. The couple stood at the desk. They had missed their connection in California, and so had arrived several hours late. Because of this, their room had been let to another family. One of the clerks was making calls, trying to find an available room in one of the many nearby hotels. He was not having any luck, but assured the couple that he would find something. The couple was growing impatient, and the children contorted on the cushions and whined that they were tired, that they wanted to go to the room. The bartender walked past them and out into the courtyard and the garden beyond. He had the next day off. He wondered what he would do.

ELLISON FOWLER lives and works in Cleveland, Ohio. More of his work may be found by visiting www.EllisonFowler.WordPress.com. *THE DISTINCTION OF THE MATURE AND THE HORROR OF THE NAIVE, AND OTHER STORIES OF YOUTH IN LIMBO* is his first collection.